GUINEA PIG

PET SHOP PRIVATE EYE

#1

Hamster and Cheese

COLLEEN AF VENABLE

ILLUSTRATED BY
STEPHANIE YUE

GRAPHIC UNIVERSE™ · MINNEAPOLIS · NEW YORK

Story by Colleen AF Venable

Art by Stephanie Yue

Coloring by Hi-Fi Design

Lettering by Zack Giallongo

Copyright © 2010 by Lerner Publishing Group, Inc.

Graphic Universe™ is a trademark of Lerner Publishing Group, Inc.

Graphic Universe™
A division of Lerner Publishing Group, Inc.
241 First Avenue North
Minneapolis, MN 55401 U.S.A.

Website address: www.lernerbooks.com

Library of Congress Cataloging-in-Publication Data

Venable, Colleen AF.
   Hamster and cheese / by Colleen AF Venable ; illustrated by Stephanie Yue.
       p.   cm. — (Guinea PIG, pet shop private eye ; #01)
       Summary: Sasspants, a guinea pig, reluctantly agrees to act as a private investigator when Hamisher the hamster begs for her help in discovering who is stealing sandwiches from the pet shop's befuddled owner.
     ISBN: 978–0–7613–4598–5 (lib. bdg. : alk. paper)
     1. Graphic novels. [1. Graphic novels. 2. Mystery and detective stories. 3. Guinea pigs—Fiction. 4. Hamsters—Fiction. 5. Pet shops—Fiction. 6. Animals—Fiction. 7. Humorous stories.] I. Yue, Stephanie, ill. II. Title.
   PZ7.7.V46Ham 2010
   741.5'973—dc22   2009020895

Manufactured in the United States of America
5 – DP – 7/1/12

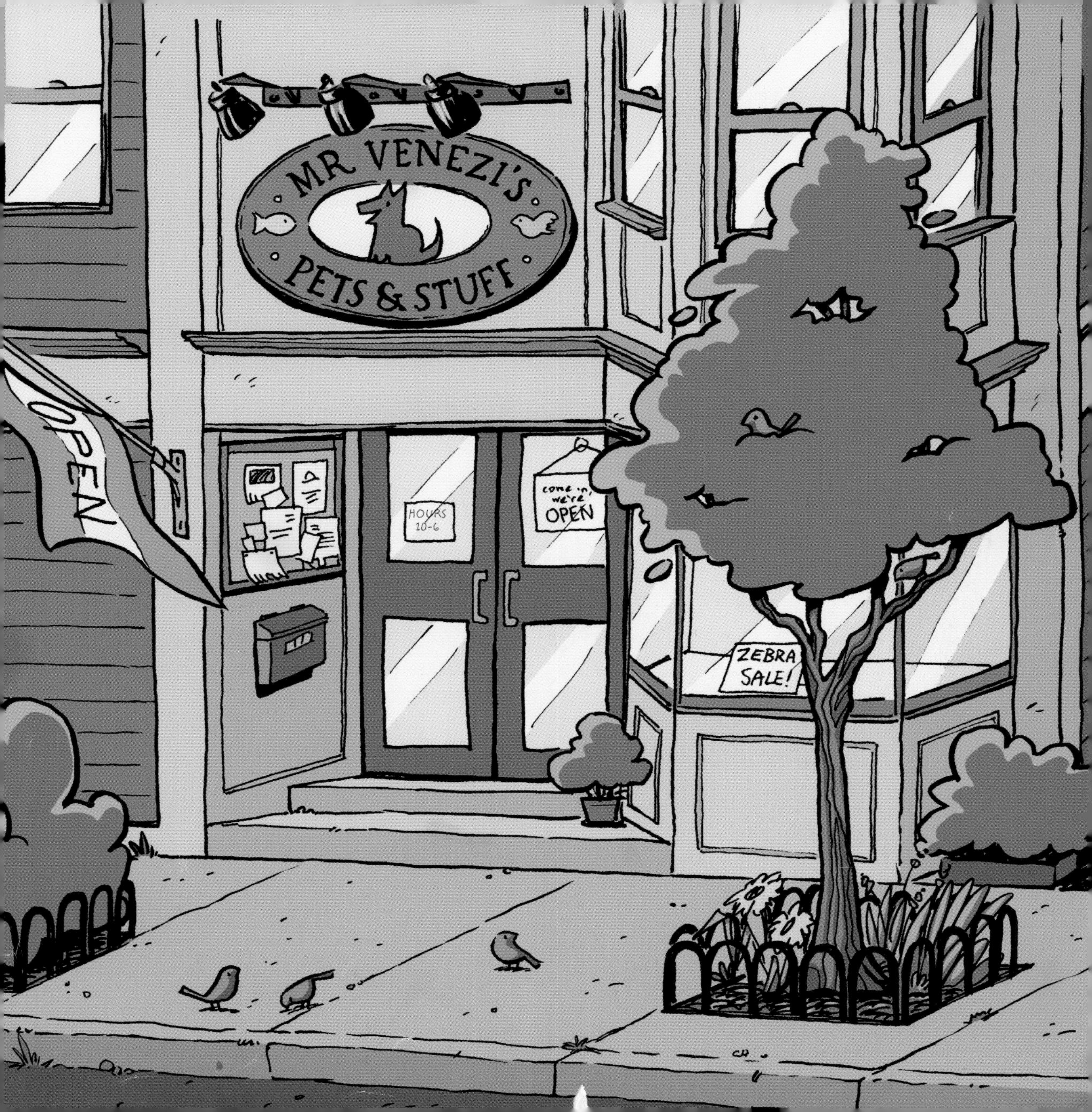
MR. VENEZI'S
PETS & STUFF
OPEN
HOURS 10-6
come in, we're OPEN
ZEBRA SALE!

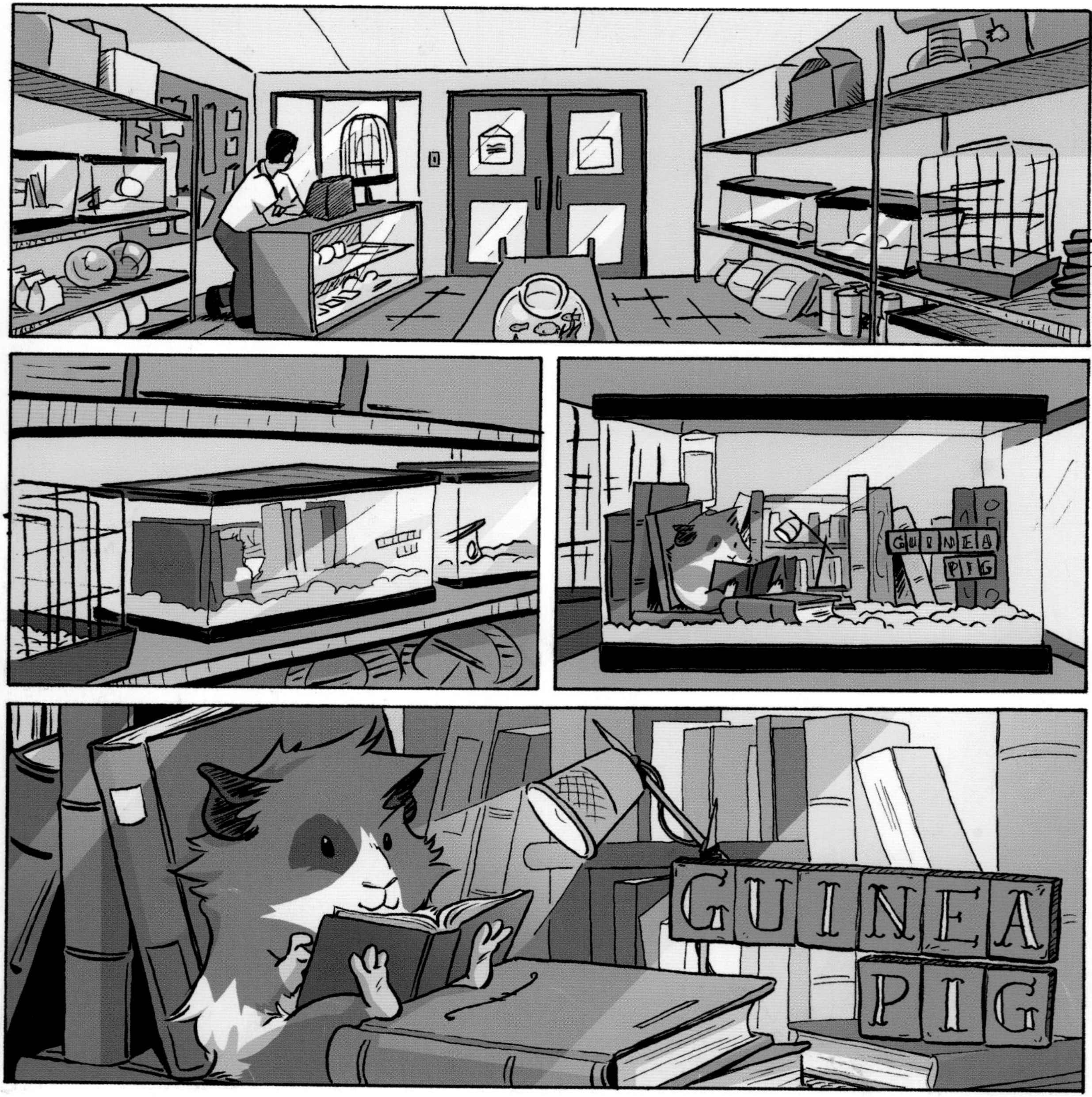
GUINEA
PIG

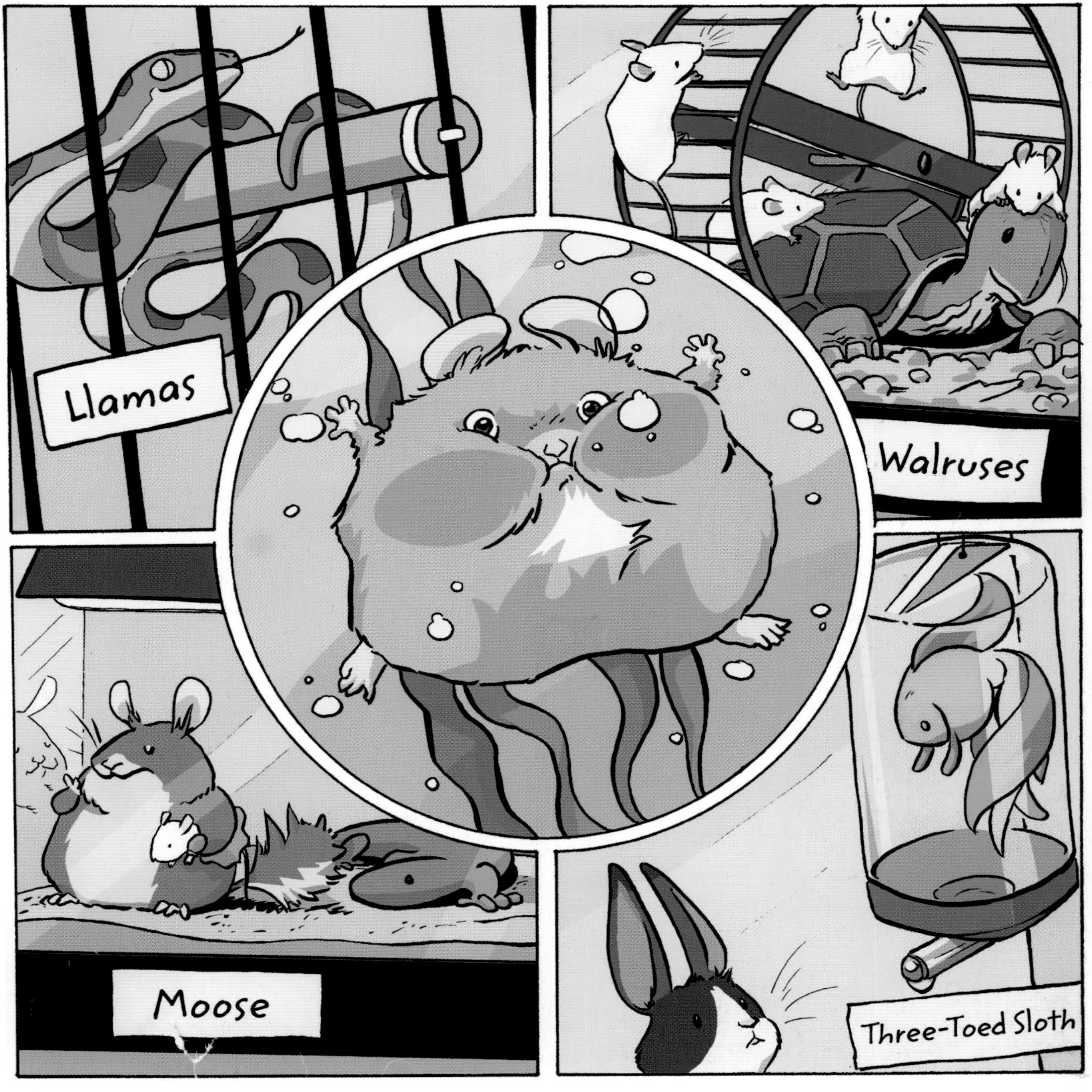
Llamas
Walruses
Moose
Three-Toed Sloth

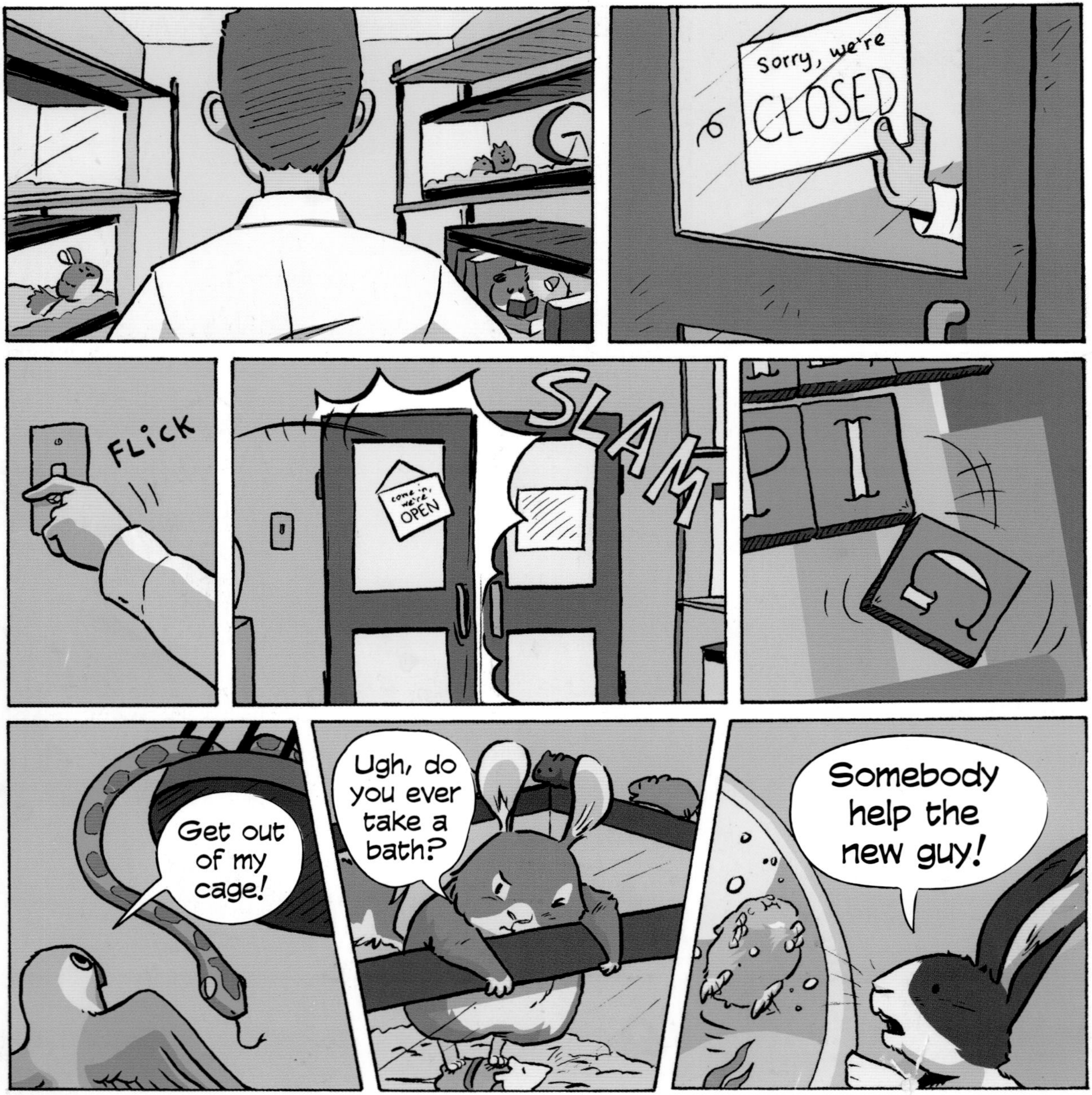
Sorry, we're
CLOSED
FLICK
come in, we're OPEN
SLAM
Get out of my cage!
Ugh, do you ever take a bath?
Somebody help the new guy!

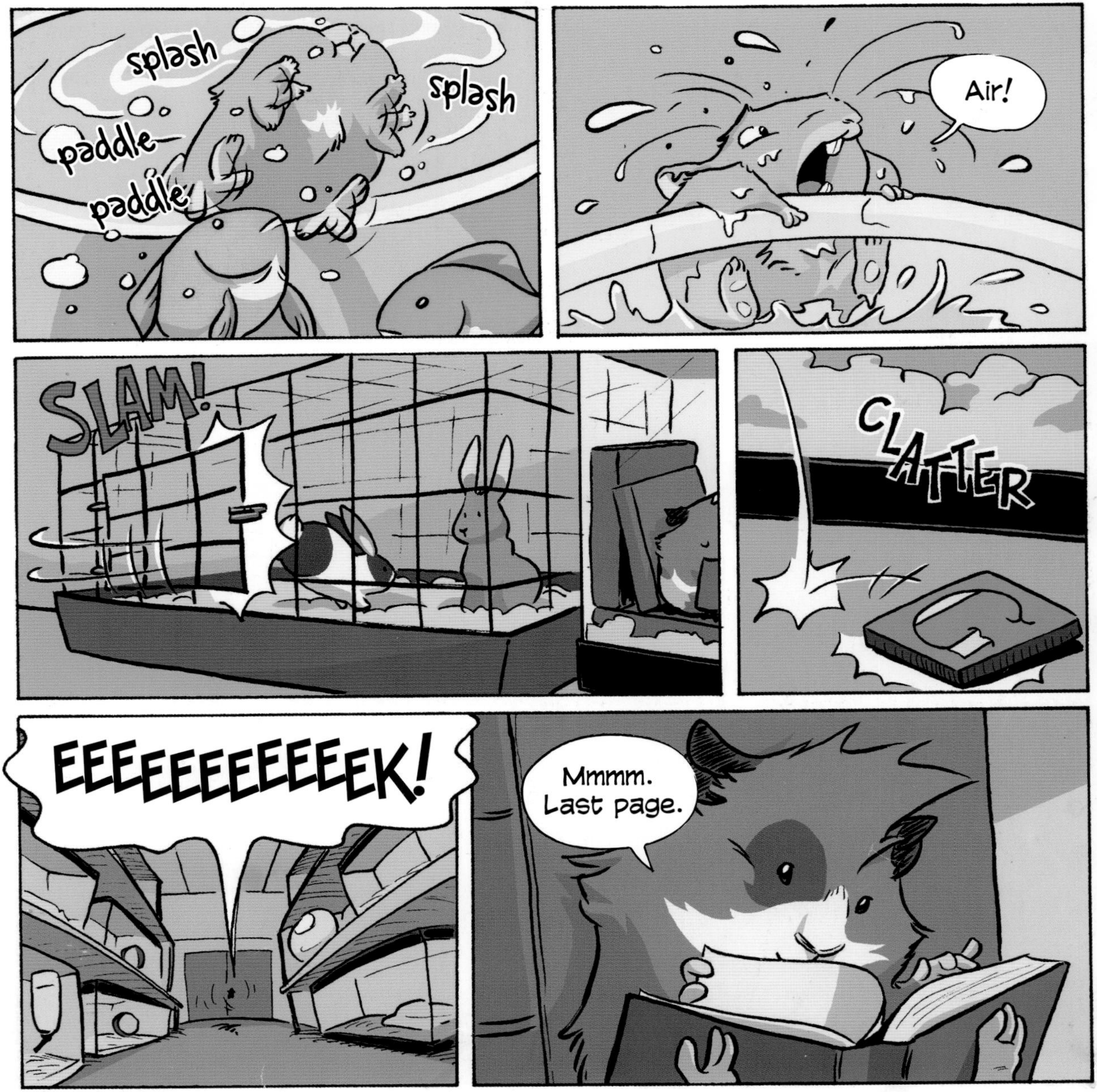
splash
splash
paddle
paddle
Air!
SLAM!
CLATTER
EEEEEEEEEEEEK!
Mmmm. Last page.

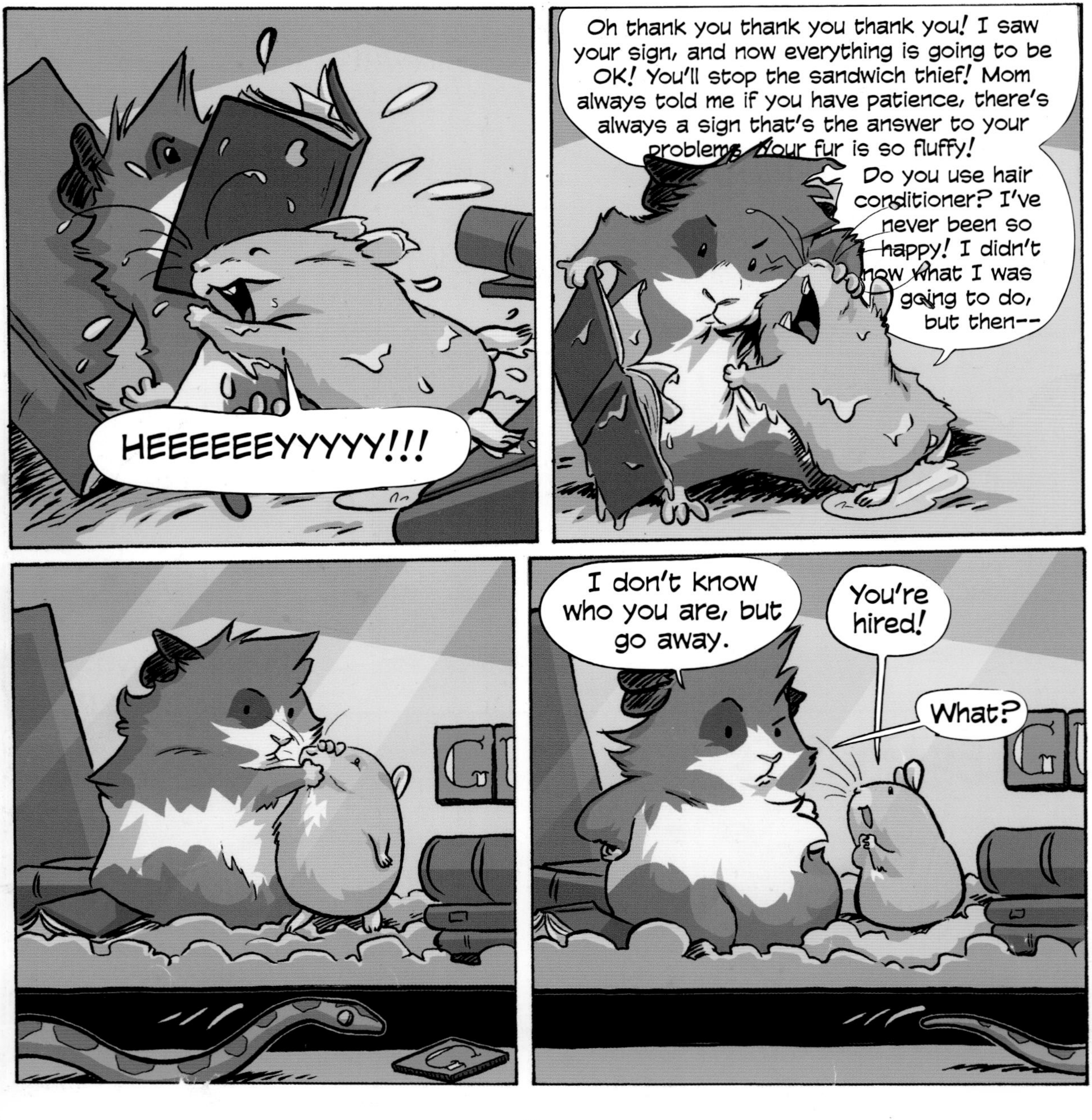
HEEEEEEEYYYYY!!!
Oh thank you thank you thank you! I saw your sign, and now everything is going to be OK! You'll stop the sandwich thief! Mom always told me if you have patience, there's always a sign that's the answer to your problems. Your fur is so fluffy!
Do you use hair conditioner? I've never been so happy! I didn't know what I was going to do, but then--
I don't know who you are, but go away.
You're hired!
What?

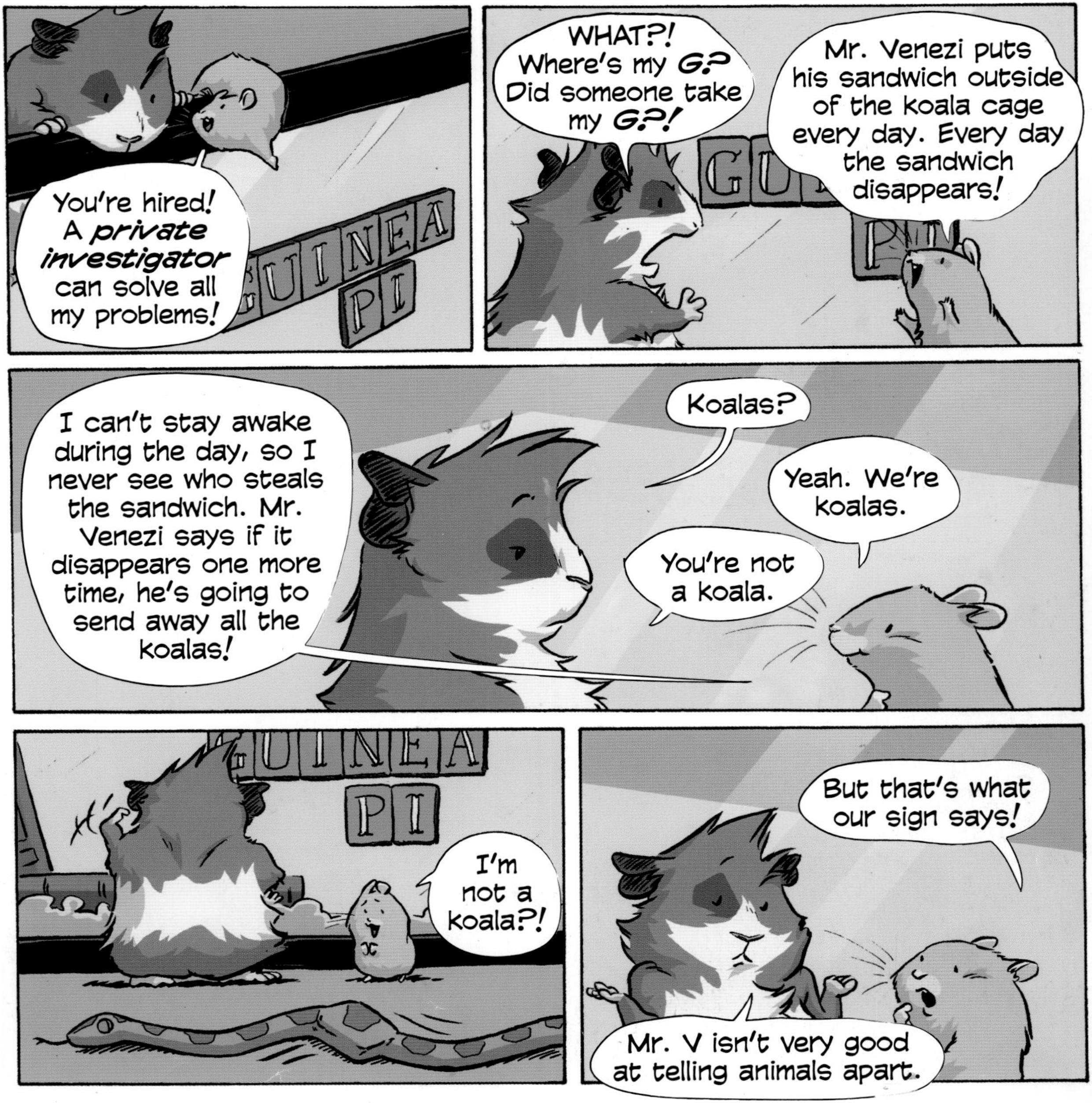
You're hired! A *private investigator* can solve all my problems!
GUINEA PI
WHAT?! Where's my *G?* Did someone take my *G?!*
Mr. Venezi puts his sandwich outside of the koala cage every day. Every day the sandwich disappears!
I can't stay awake during the day, so I never see who steals the sandwich. Mr. Venezi says if it disappears one more time, he's going to send away all the koalas!
Koalas?
Yeah. We're koalas.
You're not a koala.
UINEA PI
I'm not a koala?!
But that's what our sign says!
Mr. V isn't very good at telling animals apart.

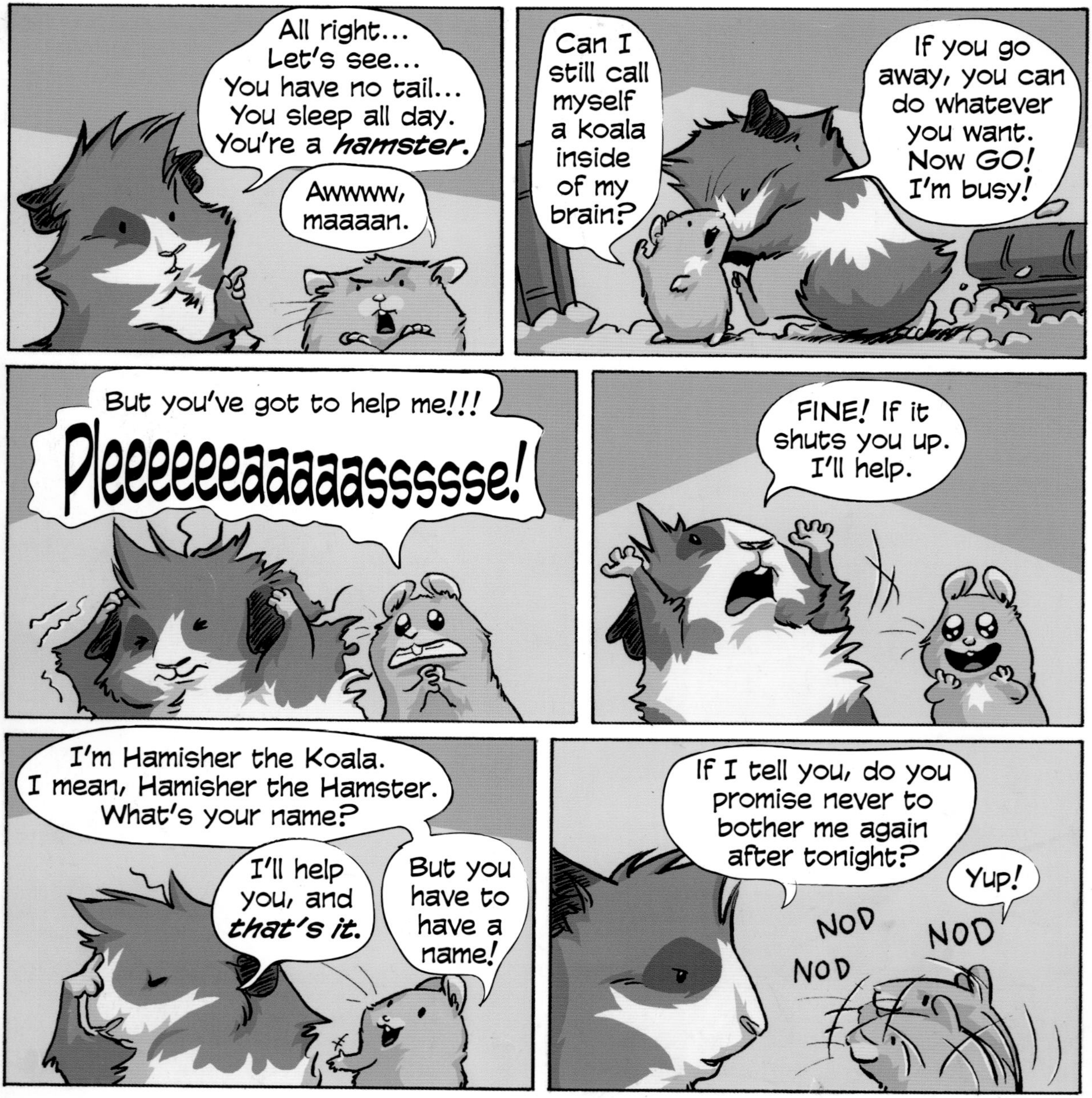
All right... Let's see... You have no tail... You sleep all day. You're a *hamster*.
Awwww, maaaan.
Can I still call myself a koala inside of my brain?
If you go away, you can do whatever you want. Now GO! I'm busy!
But you've got to help me!!!
Pleeeeeeaaaaasssse!
FINE! If it shuts you up. I'll help.
I'm Hamisher the Koala. I mean, Hamisher the Hamster. What's your name?
I'll help you, and *that's it*.
But you have to have a name!
If I tell you, do you promise never to bother me again after tonight?
Yup!
NOD
NOD
NOD

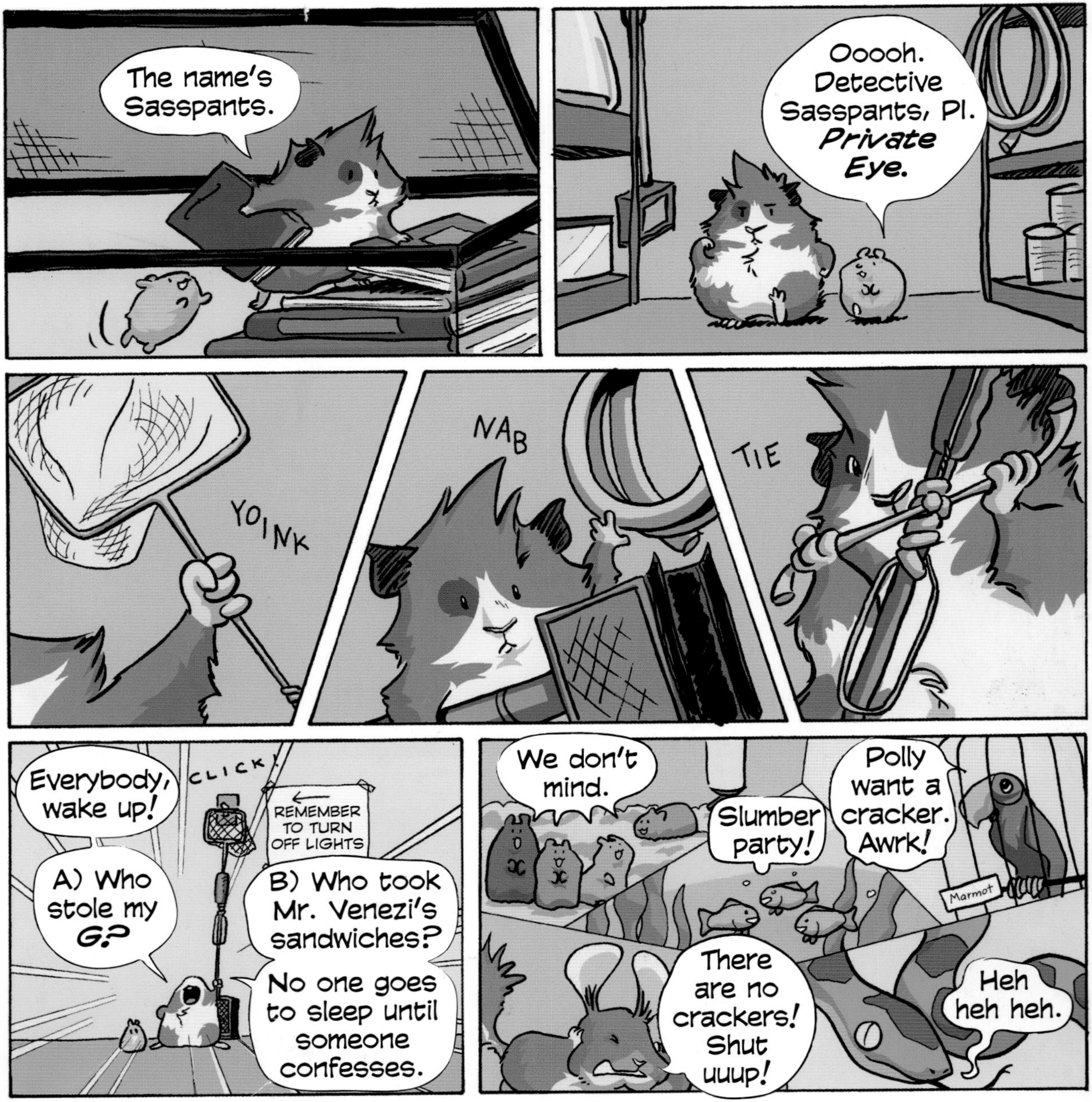
The name's Sasspants.
Ooooh. Detective Sasspants, PI. *Private Eye.*
YOINK
NAB
TIE
CLICK!
Everybody, wake up!
REMEMBER TO TURN OFF LIGHTS
A) Who stole my *G*?
B) Who took Mr. Venezi's sandwiches?
No one goes to sleep until someone confesses.
We don't mind.
Slumber party!
Polly want a cracker. Awrk!
Marmot
There are no crackers! Shut uuup!
Heh heh heh.

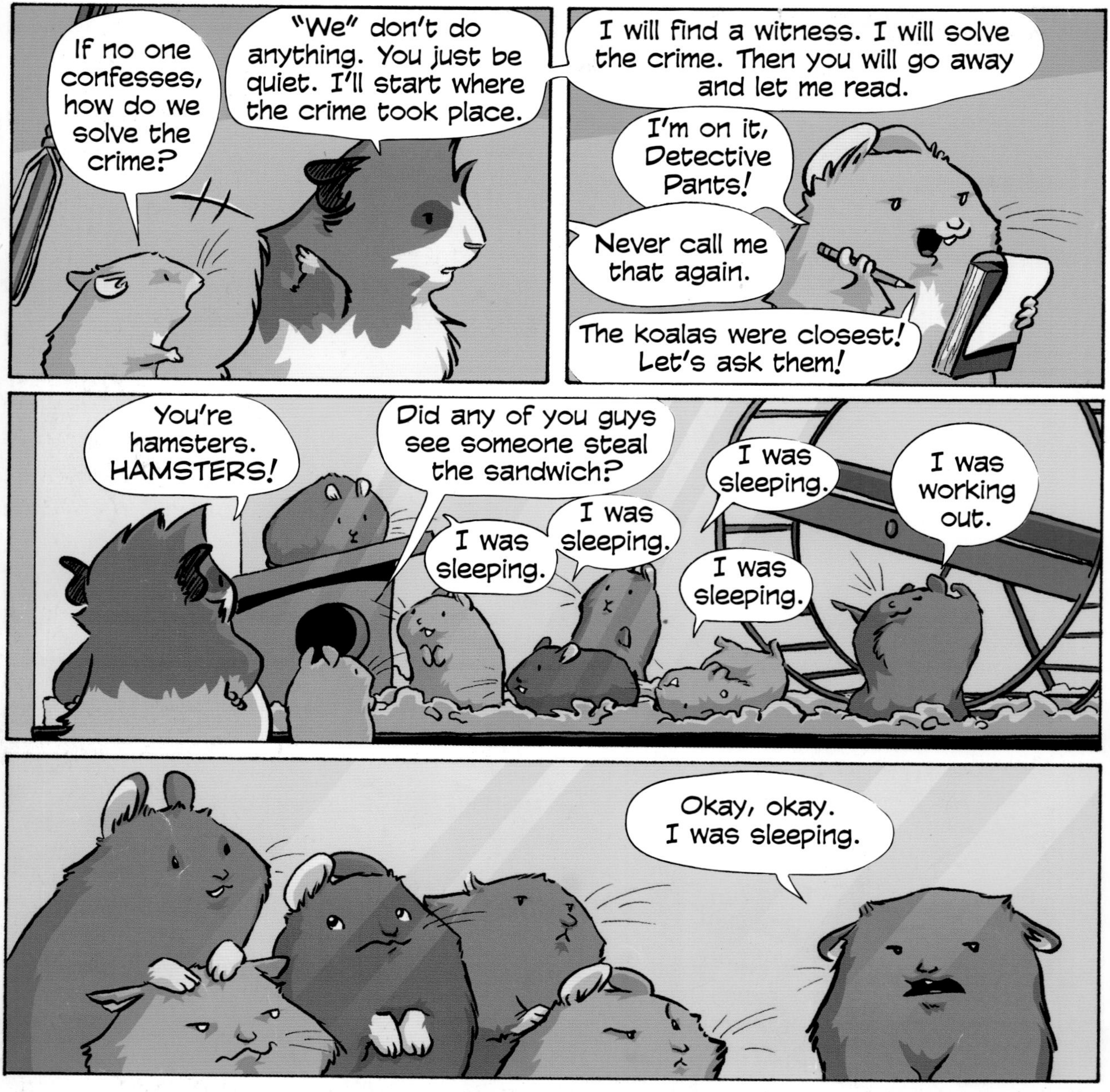
If no one confesses, how do we solve the crime?
"We" don't do anything. You just be quiet. I'll start where the crime took place.
I will find a witness. I will solve the crime. Then you will go away and let me read.
I'm on it, Detective Pants!
Never call me that again.
The koalas were closest! Let's ask them!
You're hamsters. HAMSTERS!
Did any of you guys see someone steal the sandwich?
I was sleeping.
I was sleeping.
I was sleeping.
I was sleeping.
I was working out.
Okay, okay. I was sleeping.

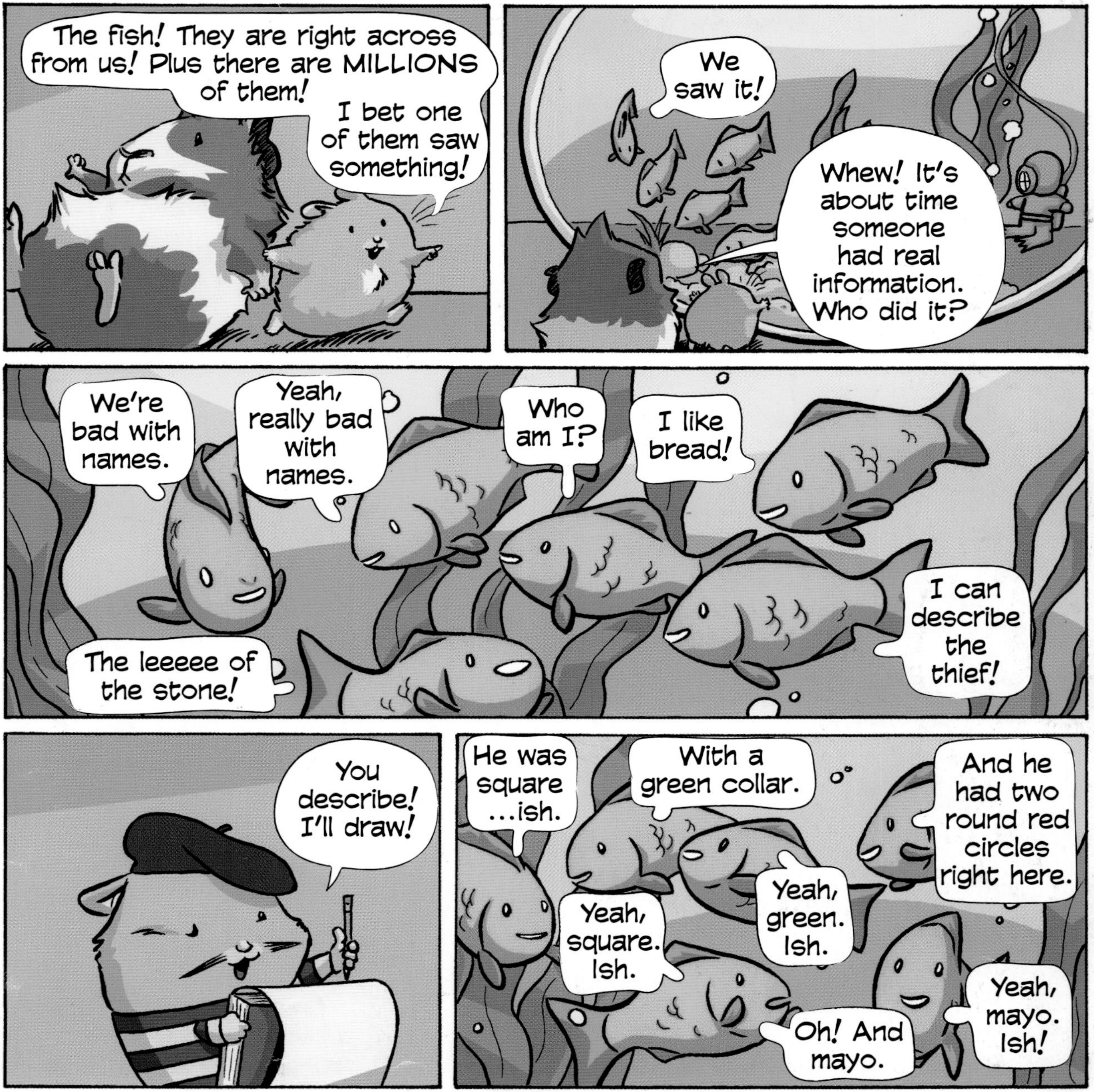

The fish! They are right across from us! Plus there are MILLIONS of them!
I bet one of them saw something!
We saw it!
Whew! It's about time someone had real information. Who did it?
We're bad with names.
Yeah, really bad with names.
Who am I?
I like bread!
The leeeee of the stone!
I can describe the thief!
You describe! I'll draw!
He was square ...ish.
With a green collar.
And he had two round red circles right here.
Yeah, square. Ish.
Yeah, green. Ish.
Oh! And mayo.
Yeah, mayo. Ish!

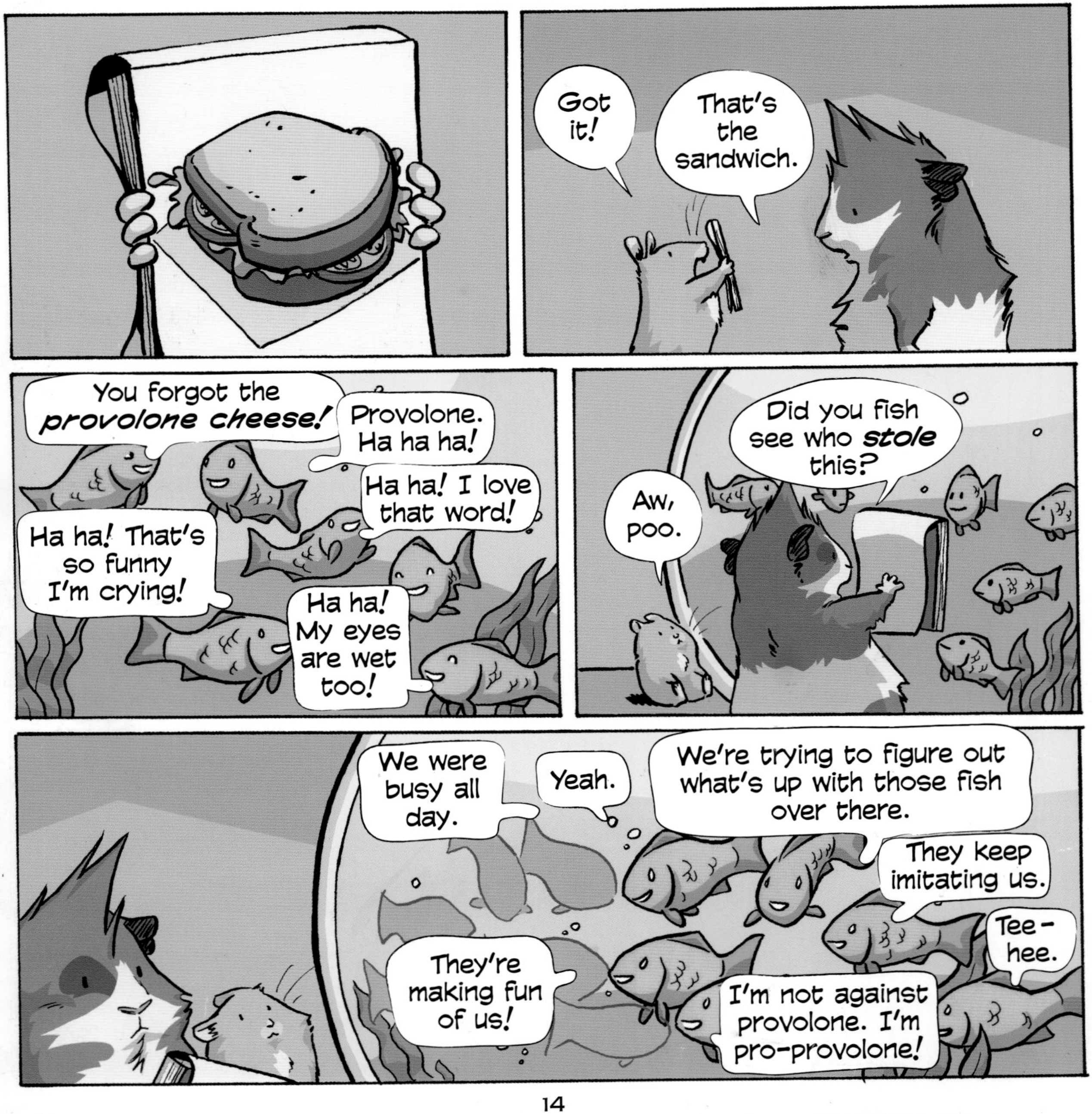
Got it!
That's the sandwich.
You forgot the *provolone cheese!*
Provolone. Ha ha ha!
Ha ha! I love that word!
Ha ha! That's so funny I'm crying!
Ha ha! My eyes are wet too!
Did you fish see who *stole* this?
Aw, poo.
We were busy all day.
Yeah.
We're trying to figure out what's up with those fish over there.
They keep imitating us.
Tee-hee.
They're making fun of us!
I'm not against provolone. I'm pro-provolone!

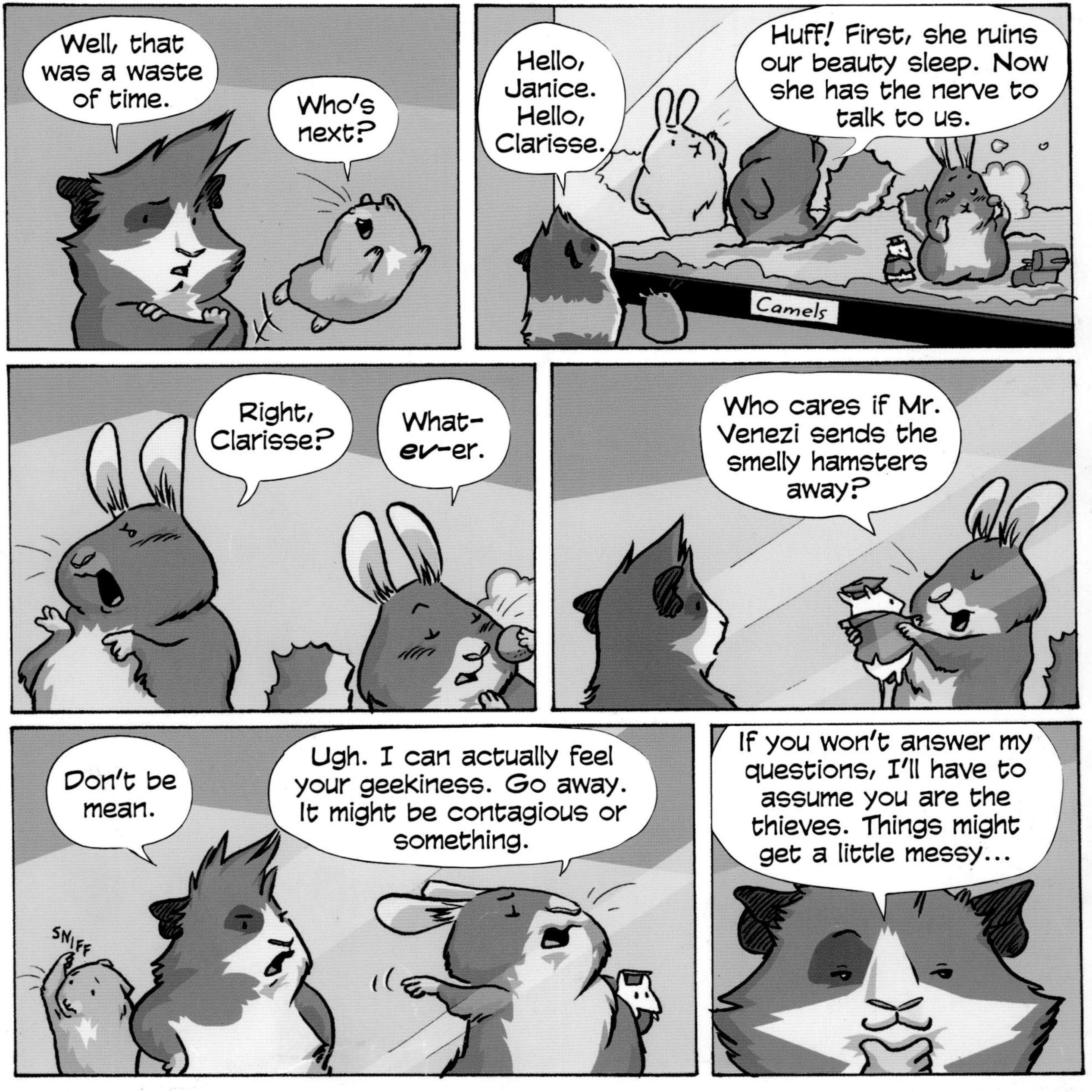
Well, that was a waste of time.
Who's next?
Hello, Janice. Hello, Clarisse.
Huff! First, she ruins our beauty sleep. Now she has the nerve to talk to us.
Camels
Right, Clarisse?
What-*ev*-er.
Who cares if Mr. Venezi sends the smelly hamsters away?
Don't be mean.
Ugh. I can actually feel your geekiness. Go away. It might be contagious or something.
SNIFF
If you won't answer my questions, I'll have to assume you are the thieves. Things might get a little messy...

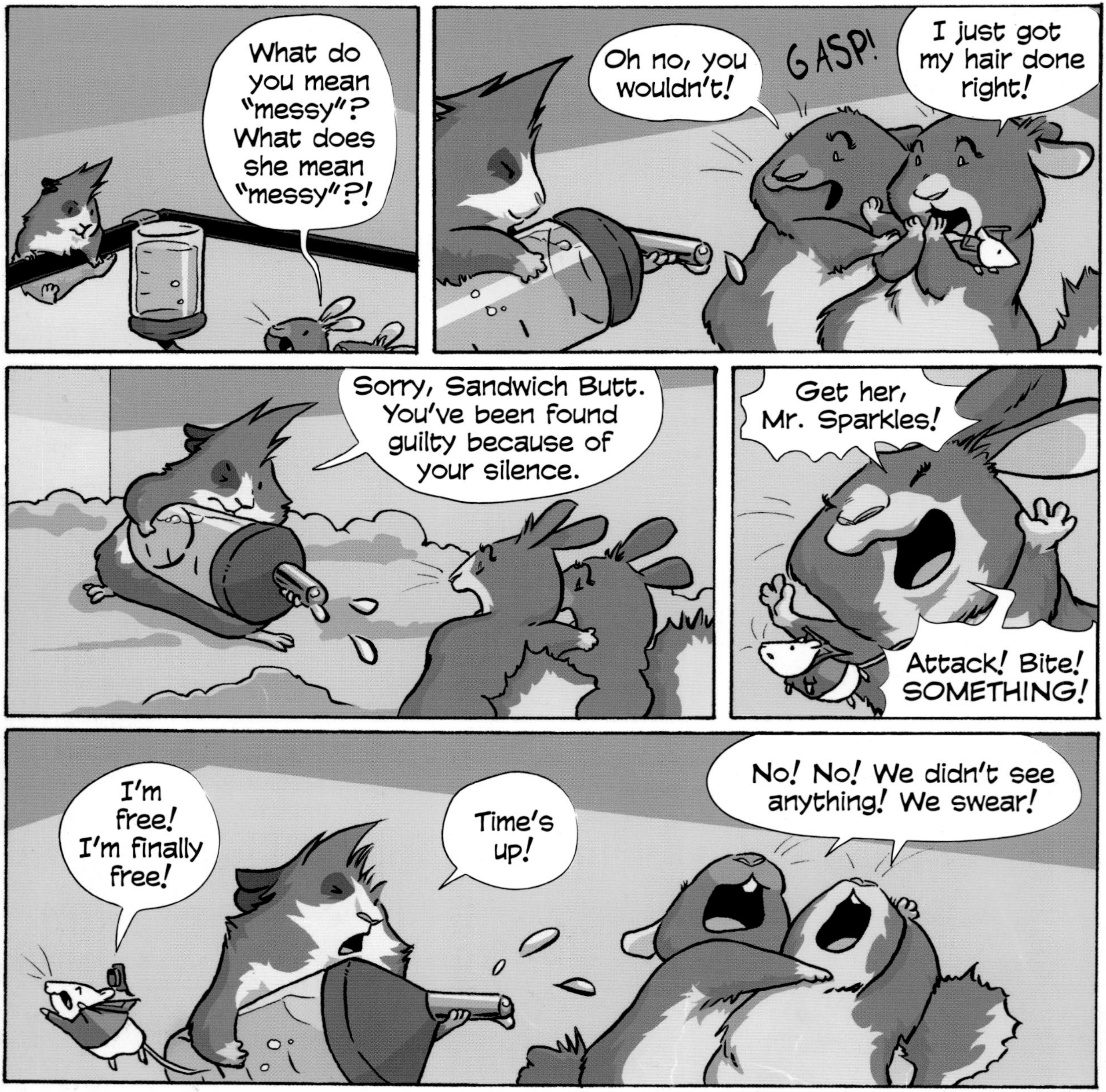
What do you mean "messy"? What does she mean "messy"?!
Oh no, you wouldn't!
GASP!
I just got my hair done right!
Sorry, Sandwich Butt. You've been found guilty because of your silence.
Get her, Mr. Sparkles!
Attack! Bite! SOMETHING!
I'm free! I'm finally free!
Time's up!
No! No! We didn't see anything! We swear!

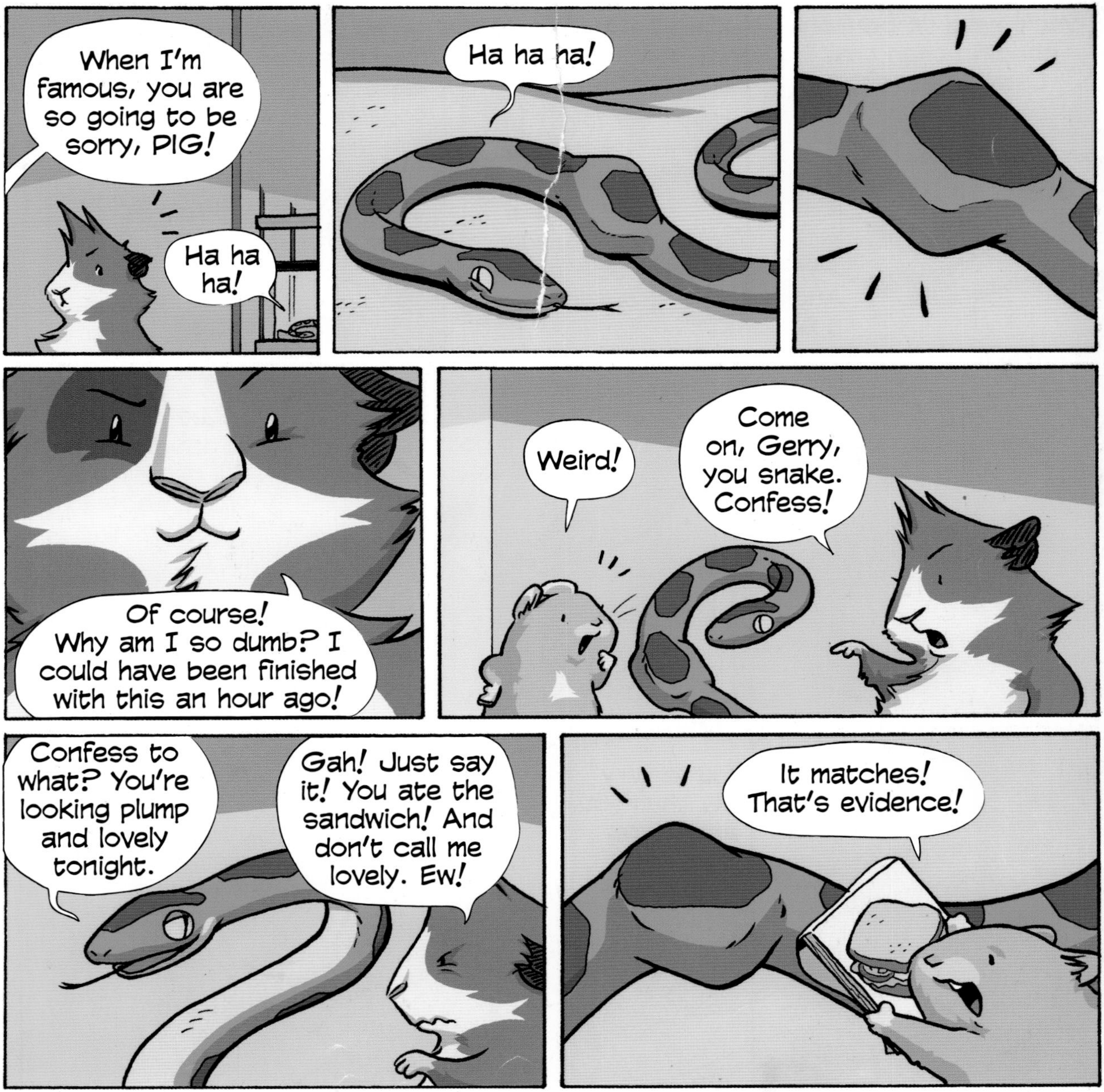
When I'm famous, you are so going to be sorry, PIG!
Ha ha ha!
Ha ha ha!
Of course! Why am I so dumb? I could have been finished with this an hour ago!
Weird!
Come on, Gerry, you snake. Confess!
Confess to what? You're looking plump and lovely tonight.
Gah! Just say it! You ate the sandwich! And don't call me lovely. Ew!
It matches! That's evidence!

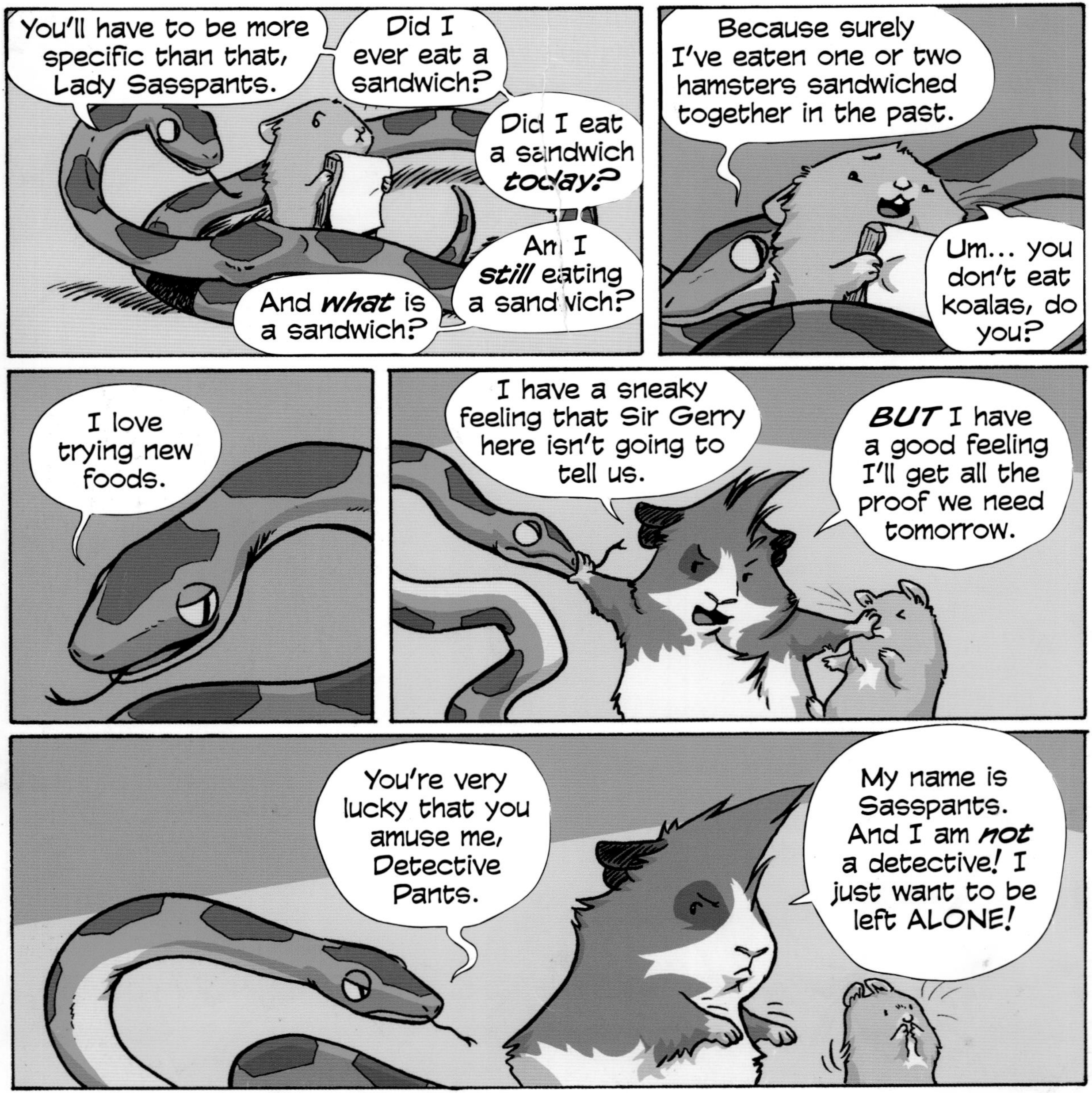

You'll have to be more specific than that, Lady Sasspants.
Did I ever eat a sandwich?
Did I eat a sandwich *today?*
Am I *still* eating a sandwich?
And *what* is a sandwich?
Because surely I've eaten one or two hamsters sandwiched together in the past.
Um... you don't eat koalas, do you?
I love trying new foods.
I have a sneaky feeling that Sir Gerry here isn't going to tell us.
BUT I have a good feeling I'll get all the proof we need tomorrow.
You're very lucky that you amuse me, Detective Pants.
My name is Sasspants. And I am *not* a detective! I just want to be left ALONE!

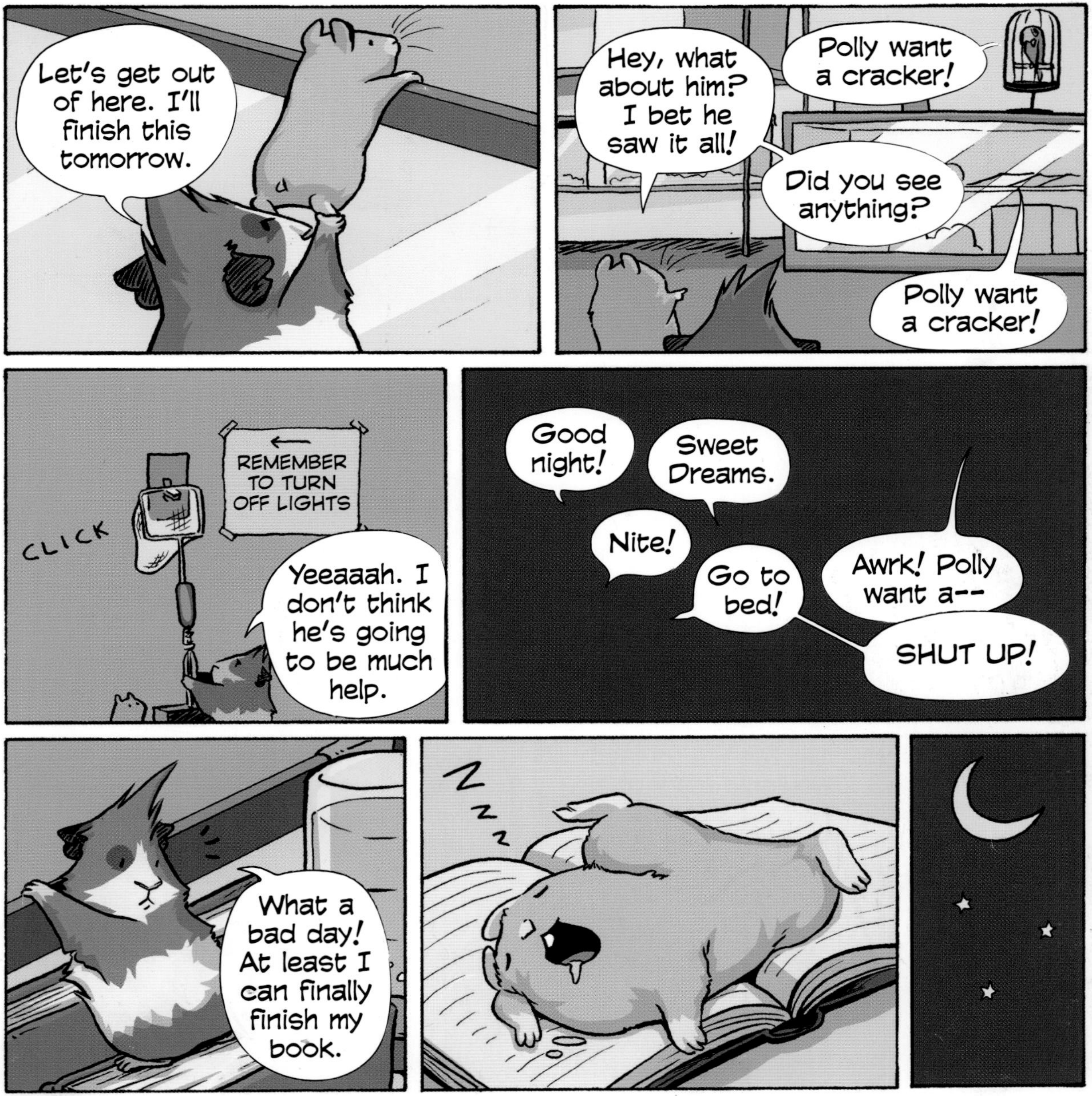
Let's get out of here. I'll finish this tomorrow.
Hey, what about him? I bet he saw it all!
Polly want a cracker!
Did you see anything?
Polly want a cracker!
REMEMBER TO TURN OFF LIGHTS
CLICK
Yeeaaah. I don't think he's going to be much help.
Good night!
Sweet Dreams.
Nite!
Go to bed!
Awrk! Polly want a--
SHUT UP!
What a bad day! At least I can finally finish my book.
Z Z Z

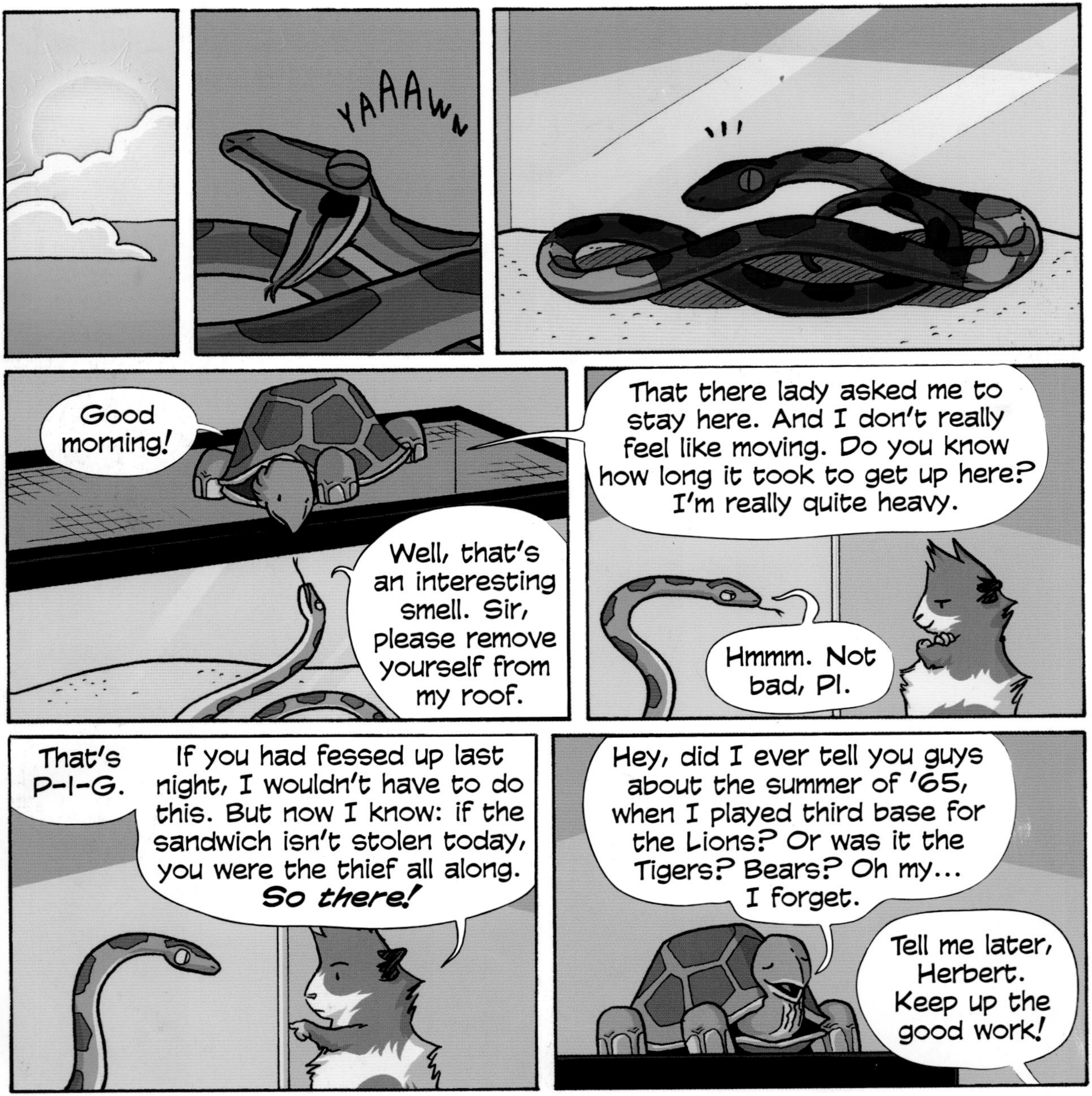
YAAAWN
Good morning!
That there lady asked me to stay here. And I don't really feel like moving. Do you know how long it took to get up here? I'm really quite heavy.
Well, that's an interesting smell. Sir, please remove yourself from my roof.
Hmmm. Not bad, PI.
That's P-I-G.
If you had fessed up last night, I wouldn't have to do this. But now I know: if the sandwich isn't stolen today, you were the thief all along. *So there!*
Hey, did I ever tell you guys about the summer of '65, when I played third base for the Lions? Or was it the Tigers? Bears? Oh my... I forget.
Tell me later, Herbert. Keep up the good work!

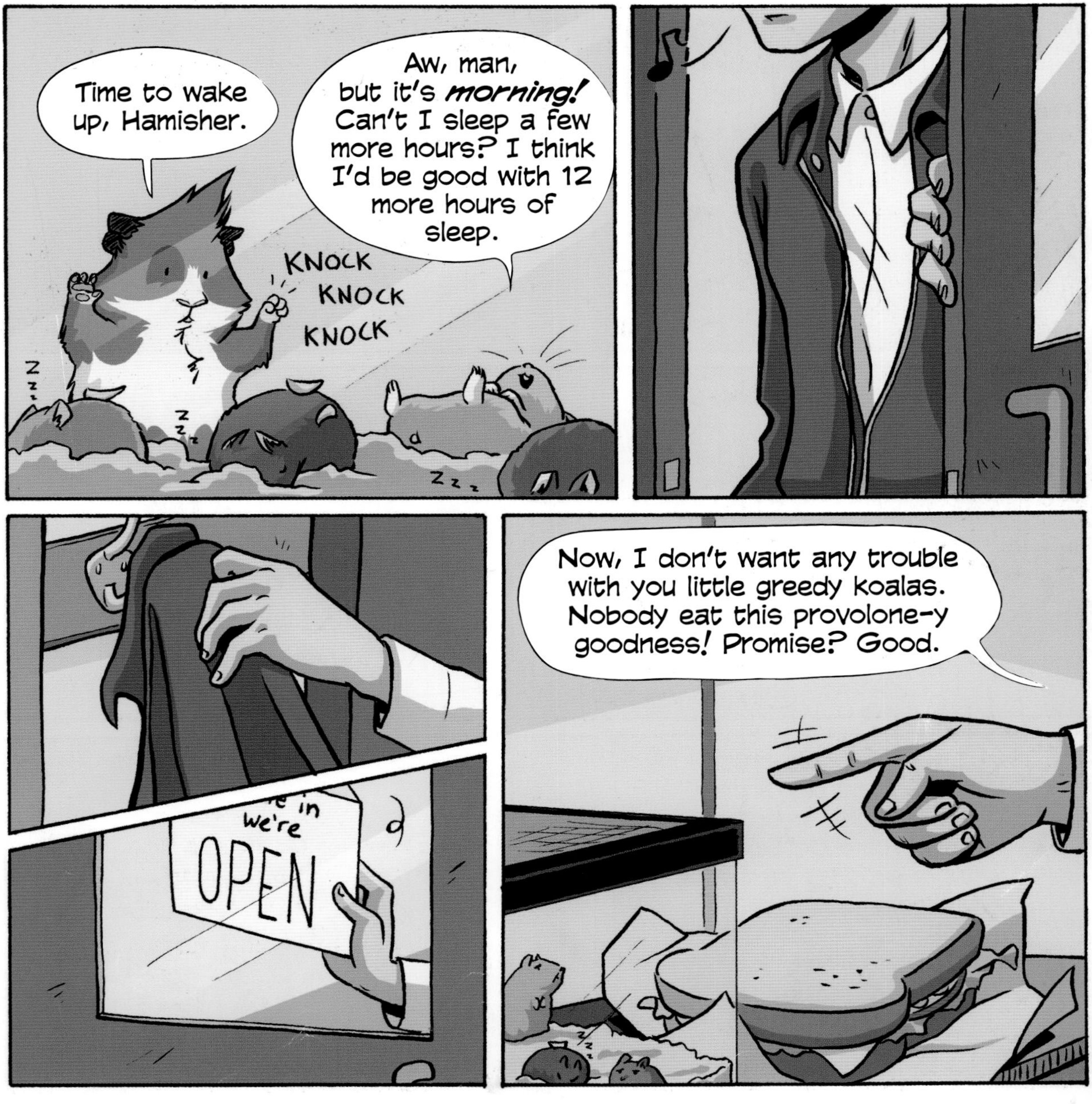

Time to wake up, Hamisher.
Aw, man, but it's ***morning!*** Can't I sleep a few more hours? I think I'd be good with 12 more hours of sleep.
KNOCK
KNOCK
KNOCK
we're
OPEN
Now, I don't want any trouble with you little greedy koalas. Nobody eat this provolone-y goodness! Promise? Good.

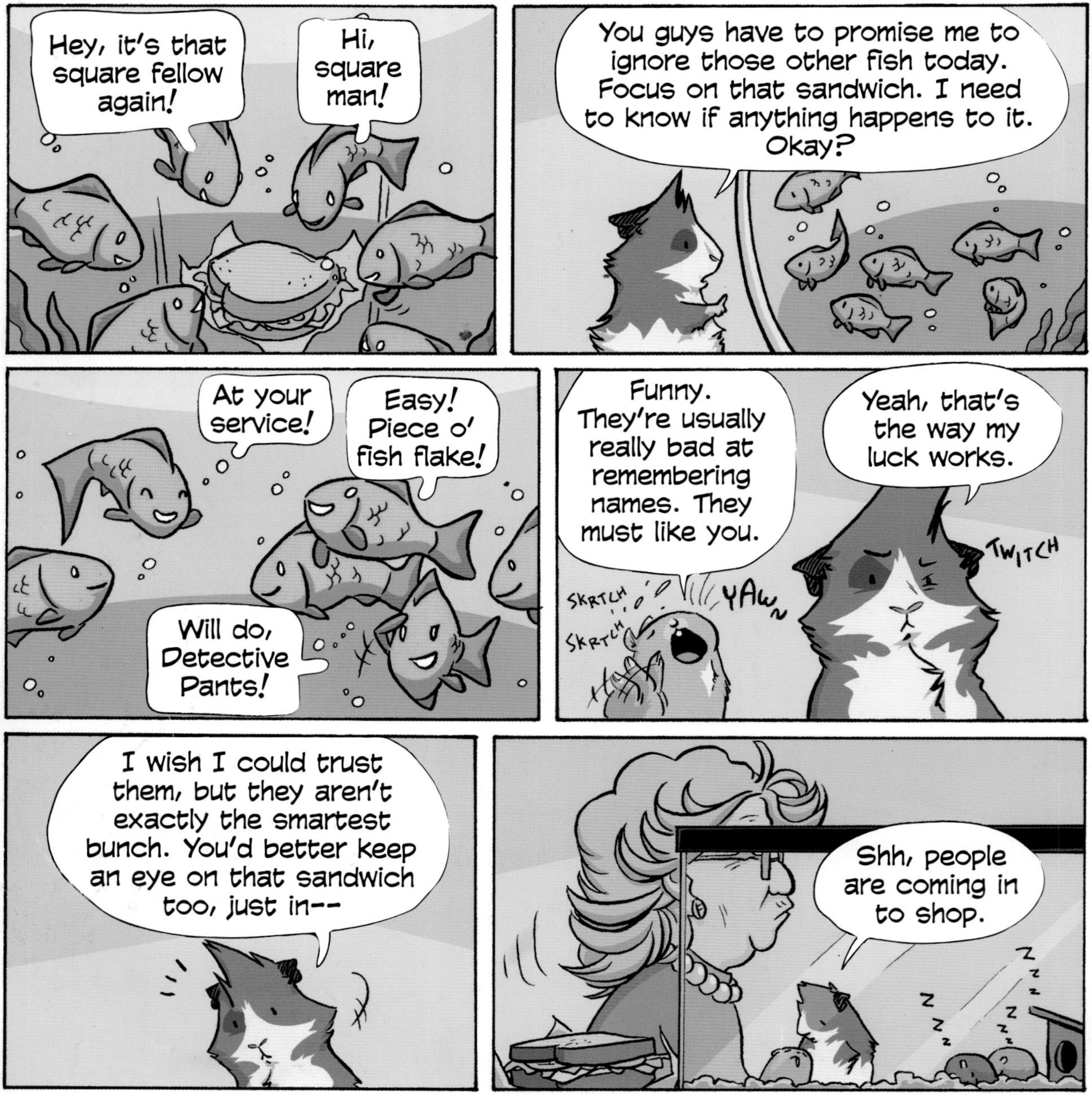
Hey, it's that square fellow again!
Hi, square man!
You guys have to promise me to ignore those other fish today. Focus on that sandwich. I need to know if anything happens to it. Okay?
At your service!
Easy! Piece o' fish flake!
Will do, Detective Pants!
Funny. They're usually really bad at remembering names. They must like you.
SKRTCH
SKRTCH
YAWN
Yeah, that's the way my luck works.
TWITCH
I wish I could trust them, but they aren't exactly the smartest bunch. You'd better keep an eye on that sandwich too, just in--
Shh, people are coming in to shop.
Z Z Z
Z Z Z

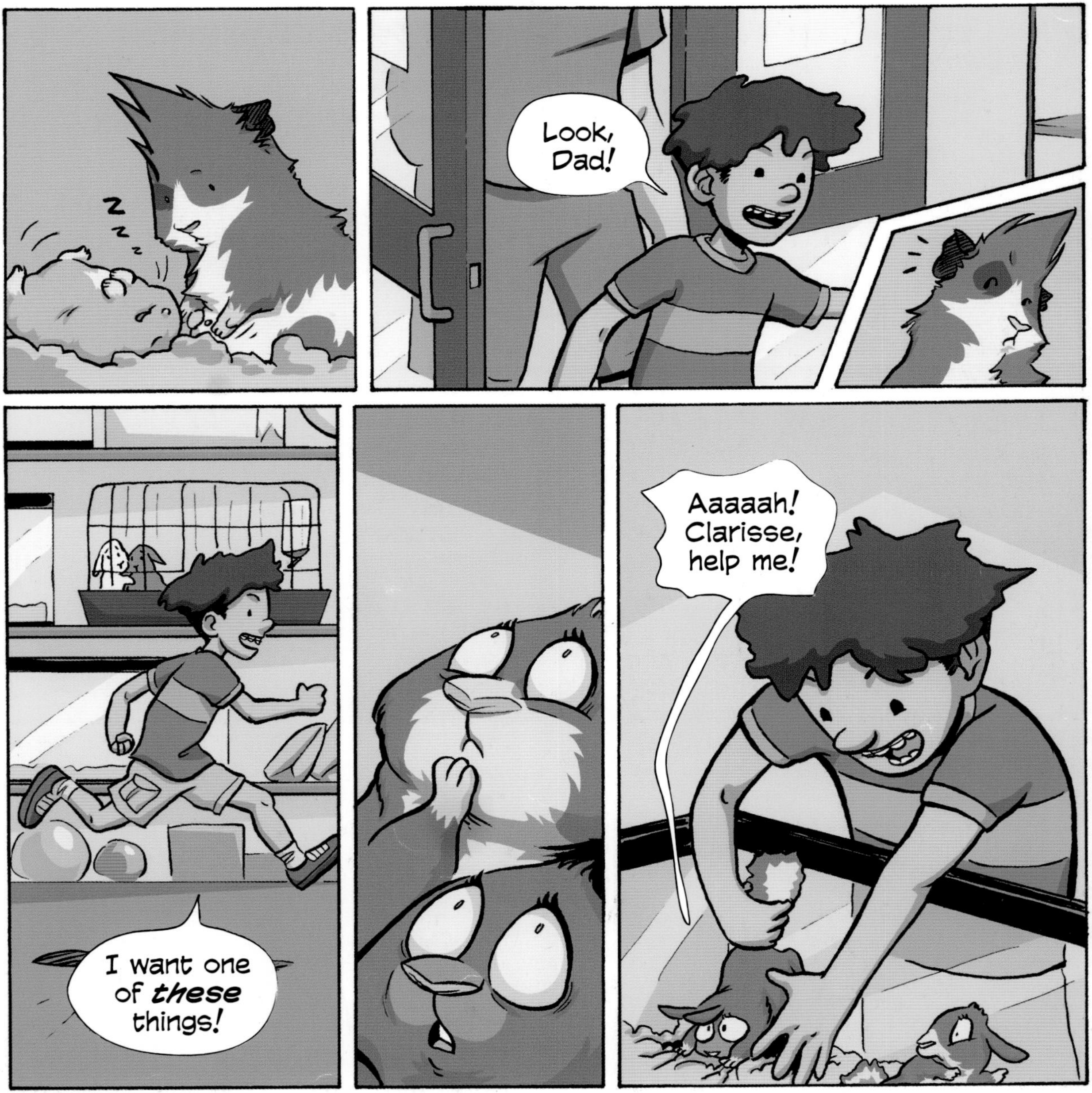
Z
Z
Z
Look, Dad!
I want one of ***these*** things!
Aaaaah! Clarisse, help me!

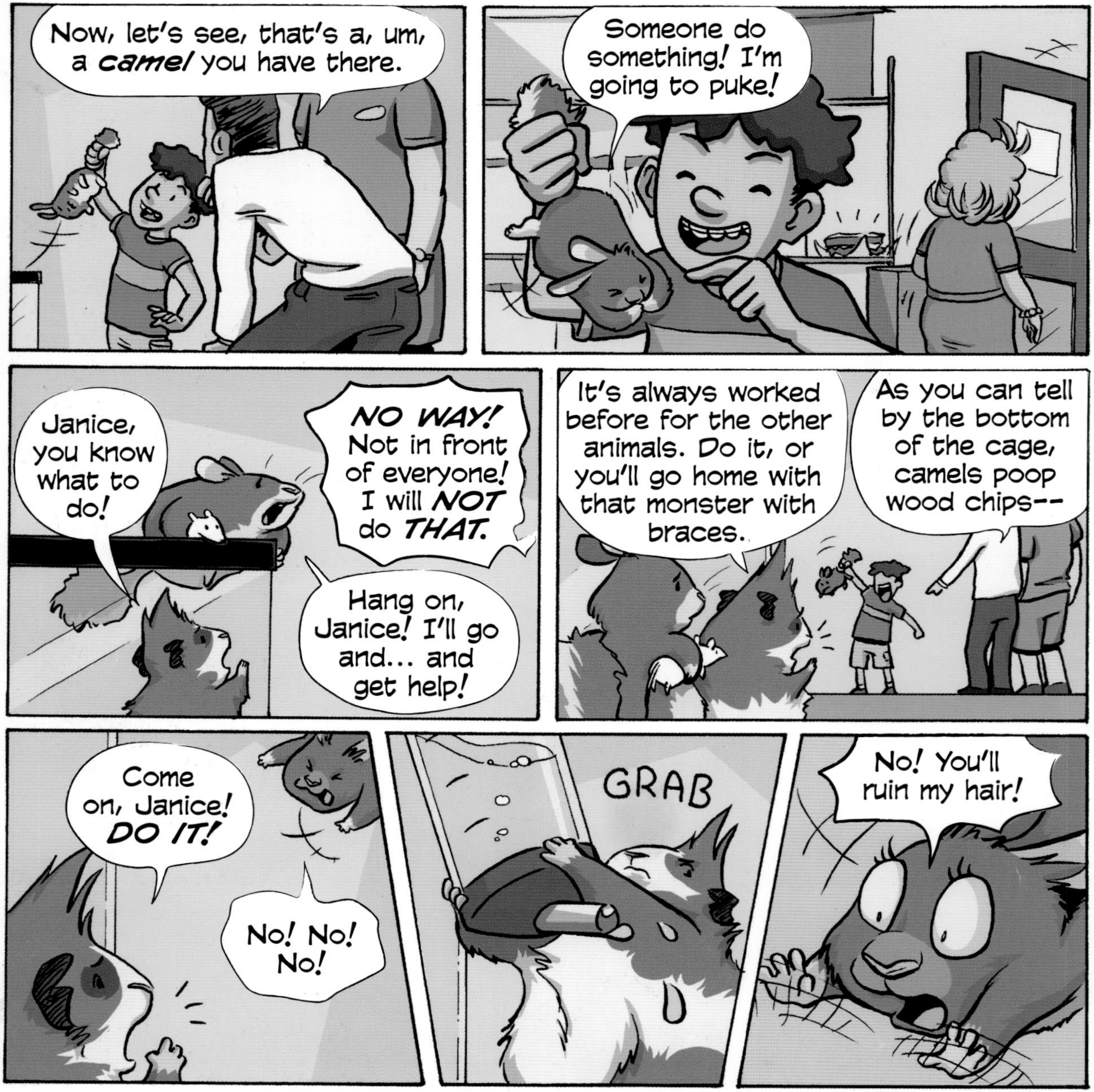
Now, let's see, that's a, um, a *camel* you have there.
Someone do something! I'm going to puke!
Janice, you know what to do!
NO WAY! Not in front of everyone! I will **NOT** do **THAT.**
Hang on, Janice! I'll go and... and get help!
It's always worked before for the other animals. Do it, or you'll go home with that monster with braces.
As you can tell by the bottom of the cage, camels poop wood chips--
Come on, Janice! **DO IT!**
No! No! No!
GRAB
No! You'll ruin my hair!

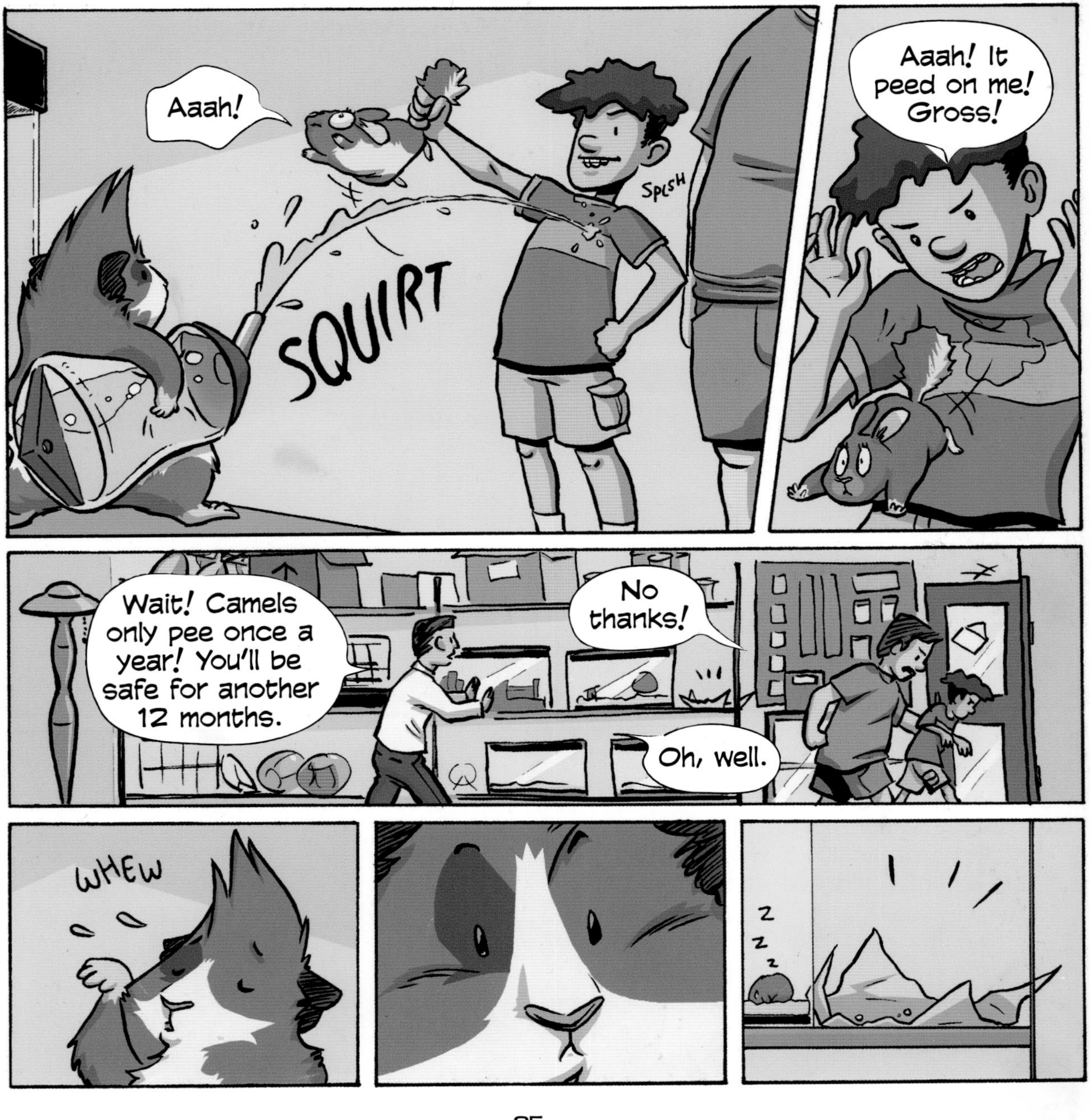
Aaah!
SPLSH
SQUIRT
Aaah! It peed on me! Gross!
Wait! Camels only pee once a year! You'll be safe for another 12 months.
No thanks!
Oh, well.
WHEW
Z
Z
Z

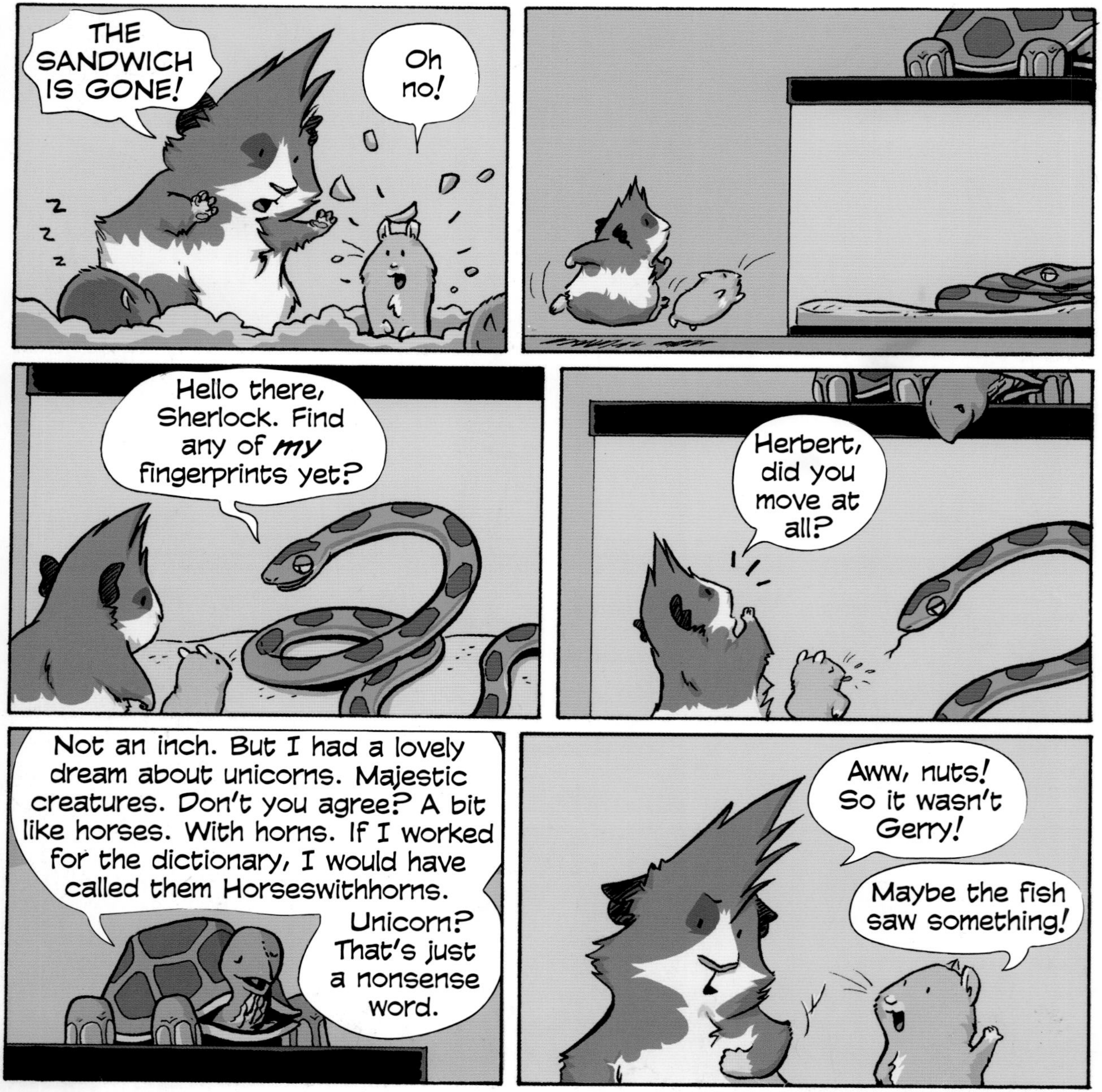

THE SANDWICH IS GONE!
Oh no!
Hello there, Sherlock. Find any of *my* fingerprints yet?
Herbert, did you move at all?
Not an inch. But I had a lovely dream about unicorns. Majestic creatures. Don't you agree? A bit like horses. With horns. If I worked for the dictionary, I would have called them Horseswithhorns.
Unicorn? That's just a nonsense word.
Aww, nuts! So it wasn't Gerry!
Maybe the fish saw something!

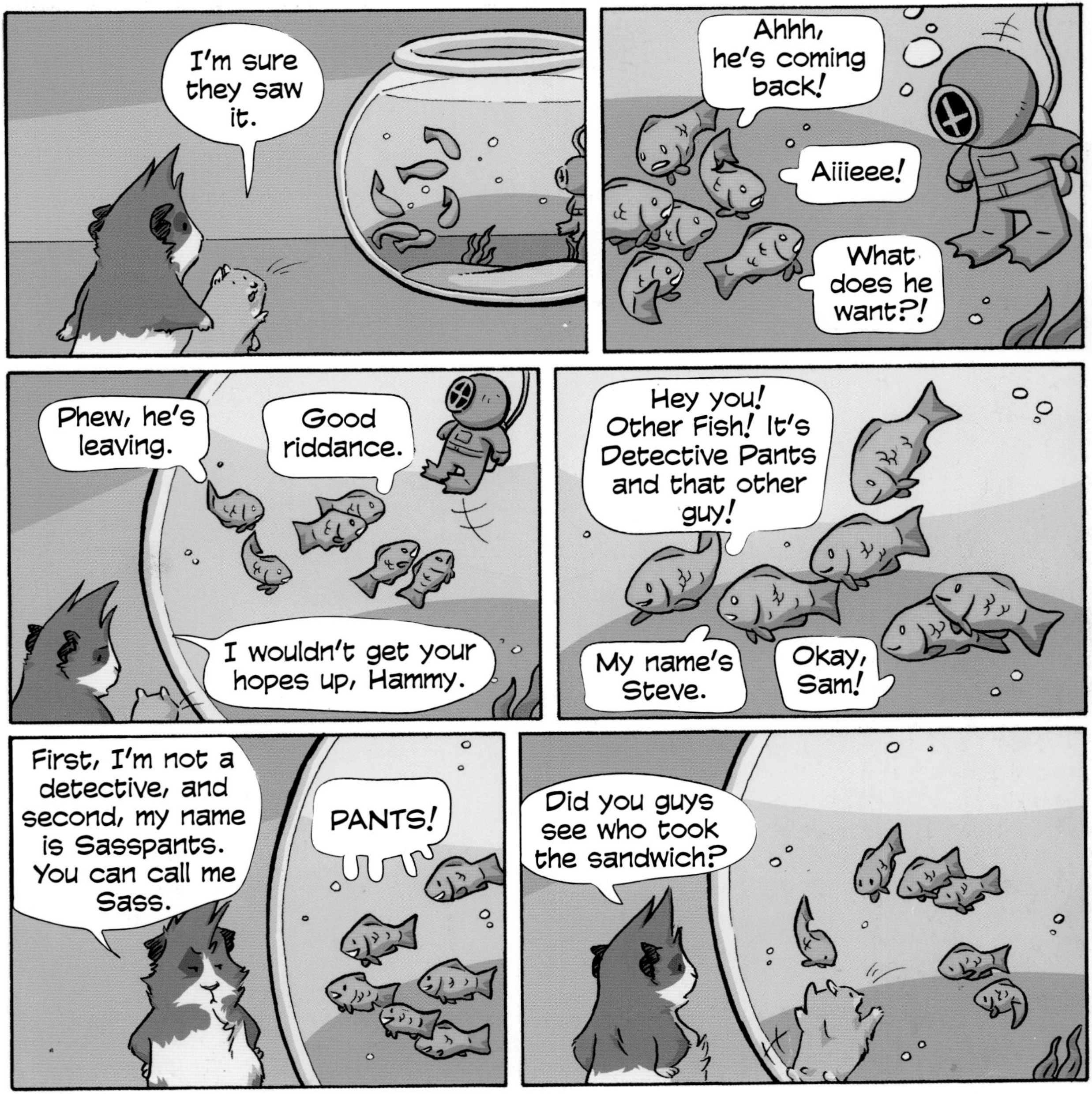
I'm sure they saw it.
Ahhh, he's coming back!
Aiiieee!
What does he want?!
Phew, he's leaving.
Good riddance.
I wouldn't get your hopes up, Hammy.
Hey you! Other Fish! It's Detective Pants and that other guy!
My name's Steve.
Okay, Sam!
First, I'm not a detective, and second, my name is Sasspants. You can call me Sass.
PANTS!
Did you guys see who took the sandwich?

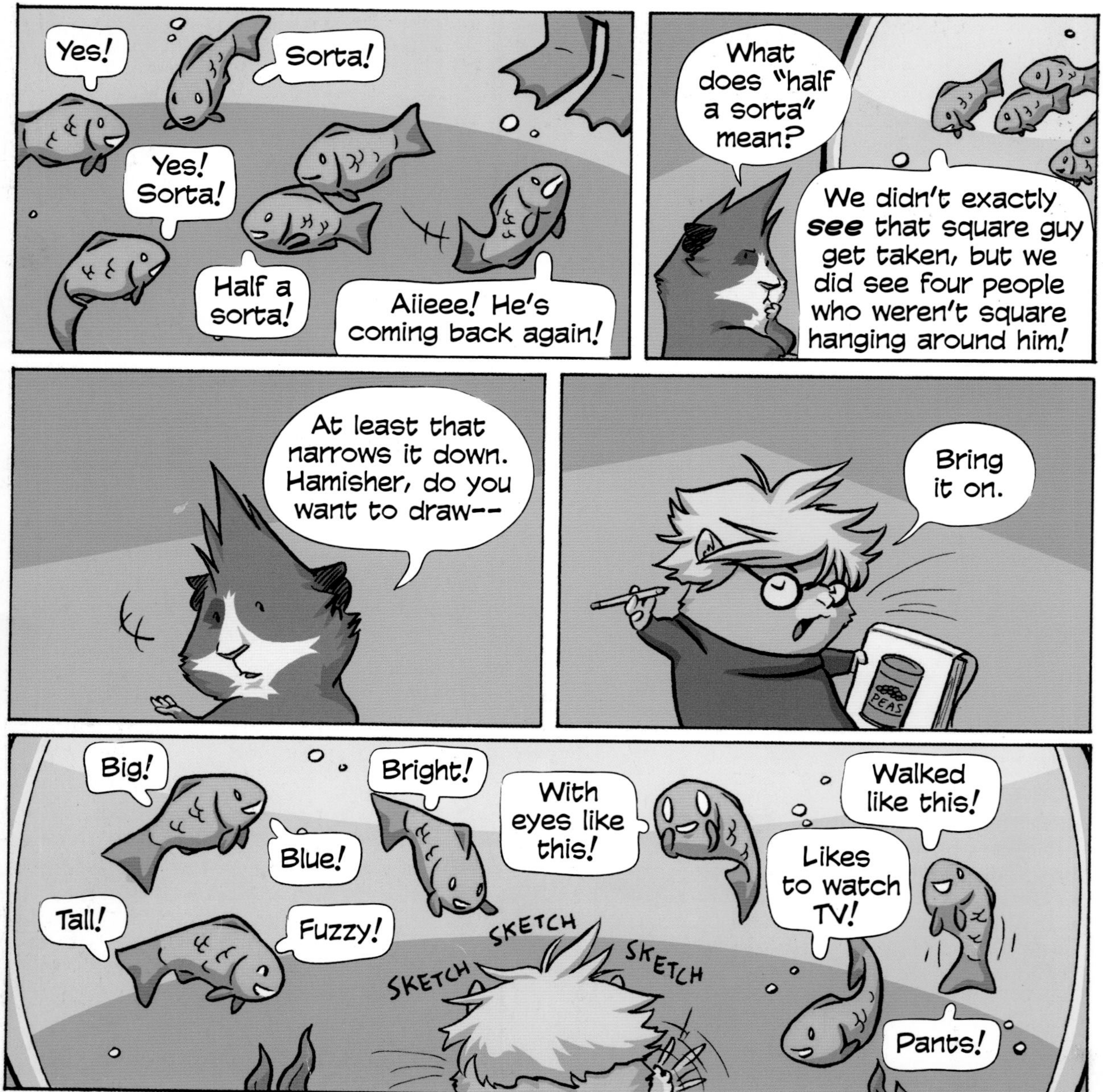
Yes!
Sorta!
Yes! Sorta!
Half a sorta!
Aiieee! He's coming back again!
What does "half a sorta" mean?
We didn't exactly **see** that square guy get taken, but we did see four people who weren't square hanging around him!
At least that narrows it down. Hamisher, do you want to draw--
Bring it on.
PEAS
Big!
Bright!
Blue!
With eyes like this!
Walked like this!
Likes to watch TV!
Tall!
Fuzzy!
SKETCH
SKETCH
SKETCH
Pants!

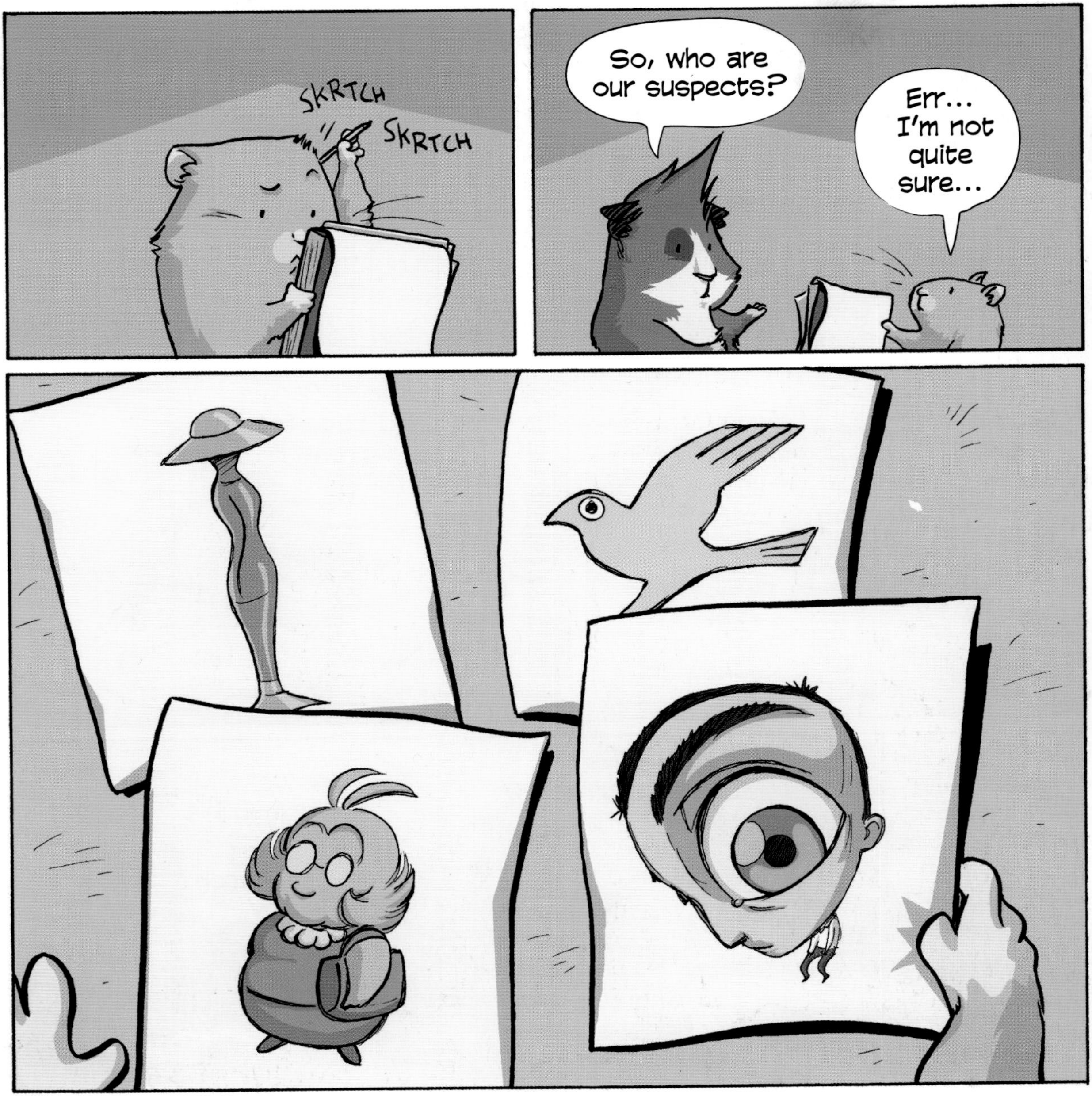
SKRTCH
SKRTCH
So, who are our suspects?
Err... I'm not quite sure...

I bet it's this guy. He looks really shifty and mean and...

How are my little kangaroos today?

Mr. Venezi. Never mind.

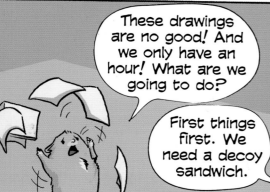

These drawings are no good! And we only have an hour! What are we going to do?

First things first. We need a decoy sandwich.

In the summer of '66, I played third base for the Tigers. Or was it the Unicorns?

Aww, now I'll never know how the story ends. Did you give up on the search?

We're almost done. You're still our prime suspect.

And I'm honored.

We're lucky Mr. V has horrible eyesight.

Wow! You look great!

I've never felt so delicious.

Hmmm. Before I start this, I should make sure the thief hasn't gotten away. Also, I don't want any more distractions.

This will keep the door shut.

JAM

HEY!

WHOOSH!

WHOOSH!

HEY!

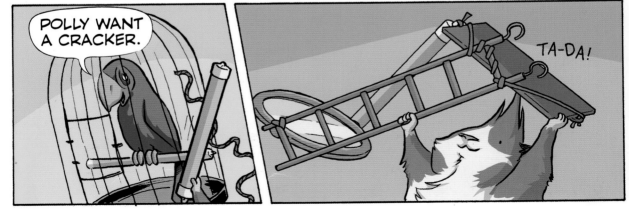

POLLY WANT A CRACKER.

TA-DA!

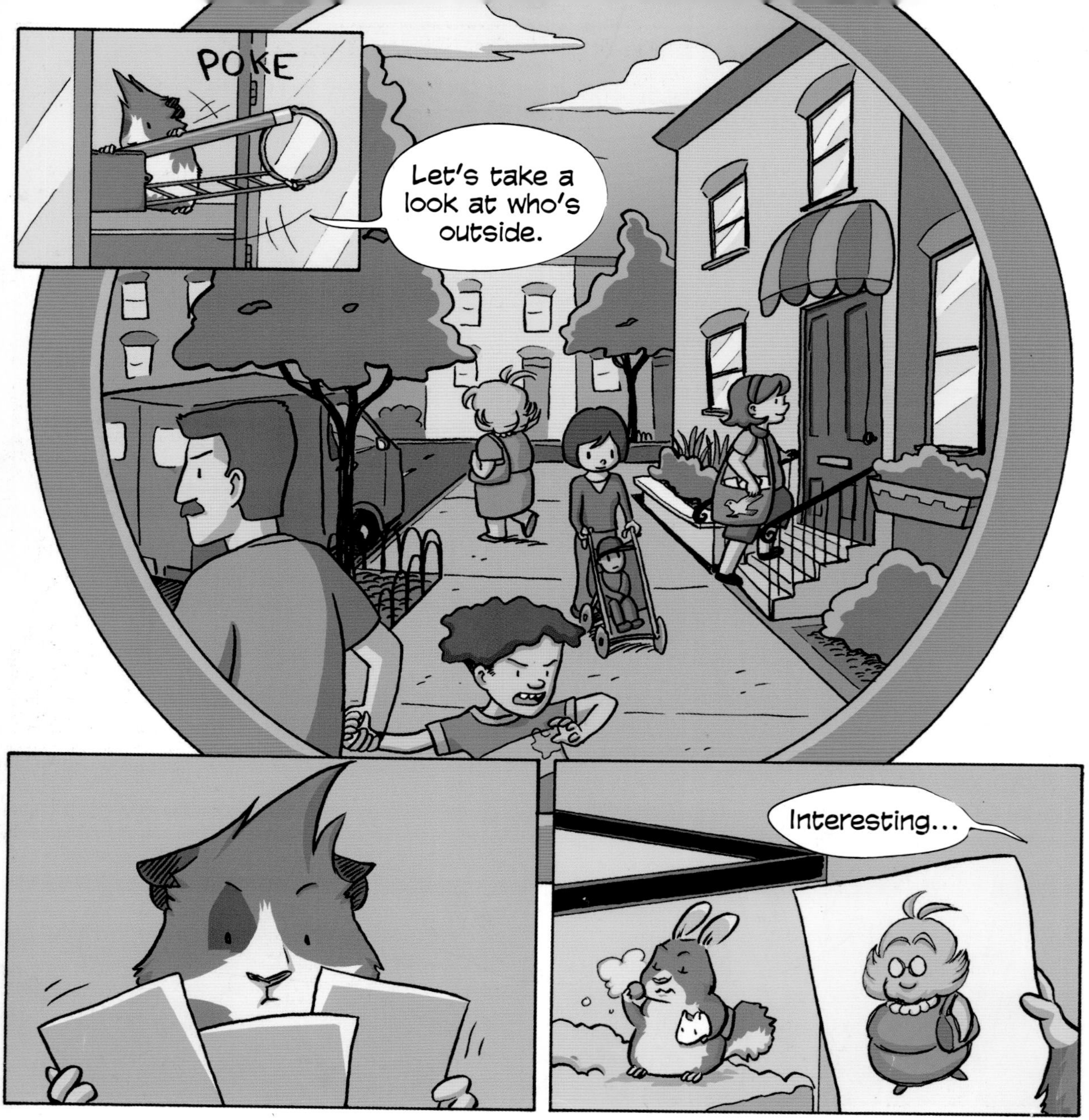
POKE
Let's take a look at who's outside.
Interesting...

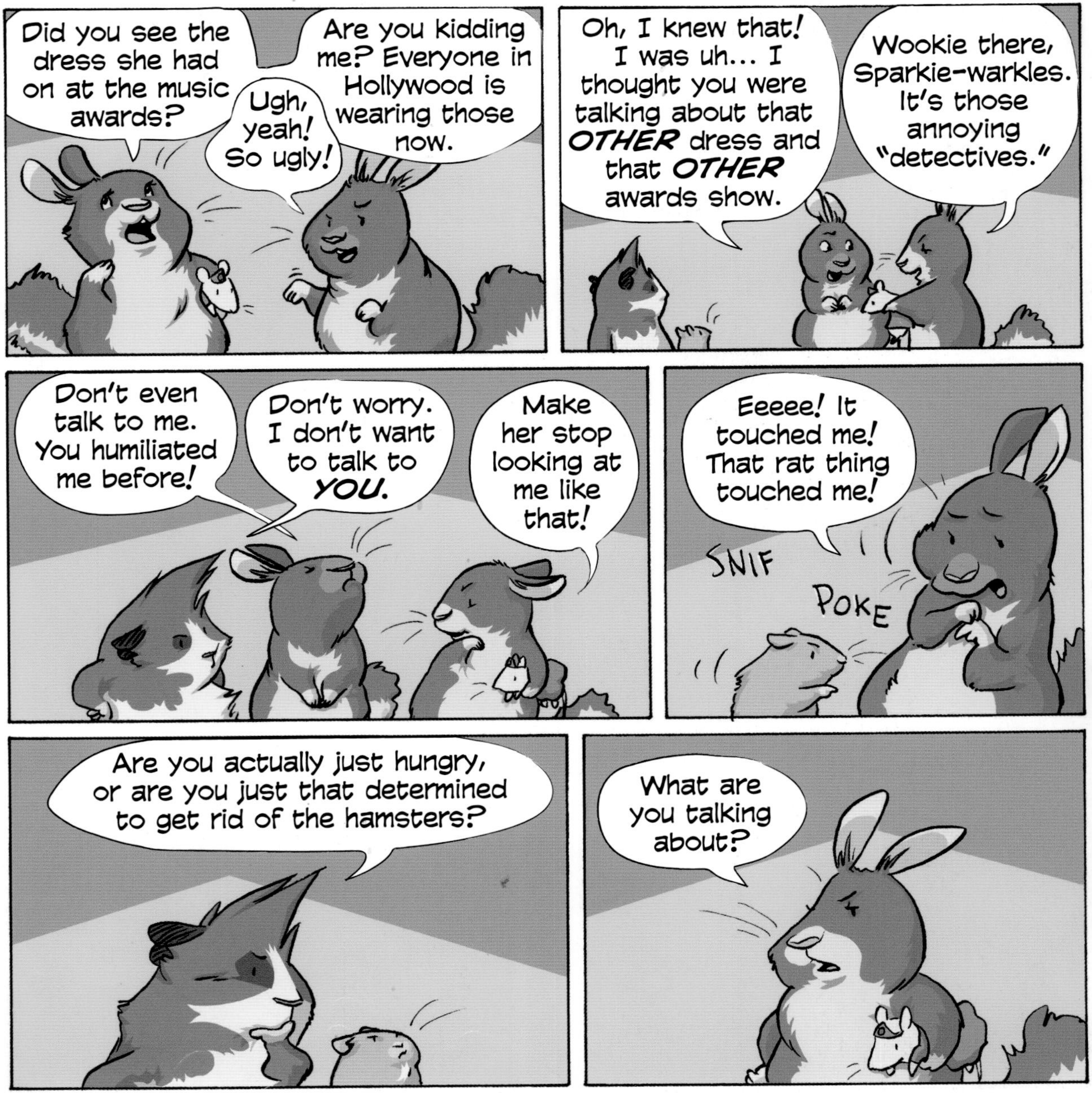
Did you see the dress she had on at the music awards?
Are you kidding me? Everyone in Hollywood is wearing those now.
Ugh, yeah! So ugly!
Oh, I knew that! I was uh... I thought you were talking about that OTHER dress and that OTHER awards show.
Wookie there, Sparkie-warkles. It's those annoying "detectives."
Don't even talk to me. You humiliated me before!
Don't worry. I don't want to talk to YOU.
Make her stop looking at me like that!
Eeeee! It touched me! That rat thing touched me!
SNIF
POKE
Are you actually just hungry, or are you just that determined to get rid of the hamsters?
What are you talking about?

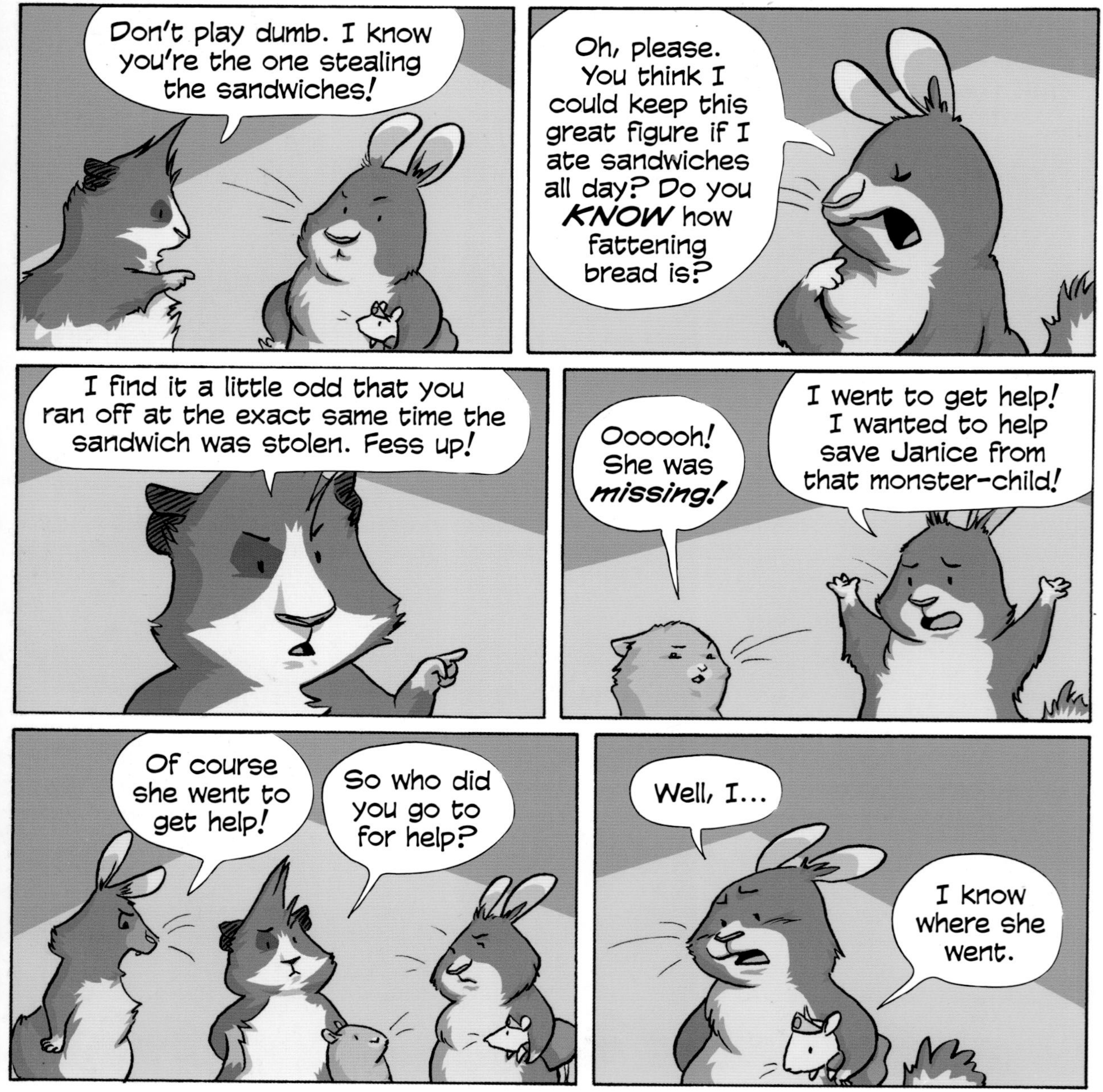
Don't play dumb. I know you're the one stealing the sandwiches!
Oh, please. You think I could keep this great figure if I ate sandwiches all day? Do you ***KNOW*** how fattening bread is?
I find it a little odd that you ran off at the exact same time the sandwich was stolen. Fess up!
Oooooh! She was ***missing!***
I went to get help! I wanted to help save Janice from that monster-child!
Of course she went to get help!
So who did you go to for help?
Well, I...
I know where she went.

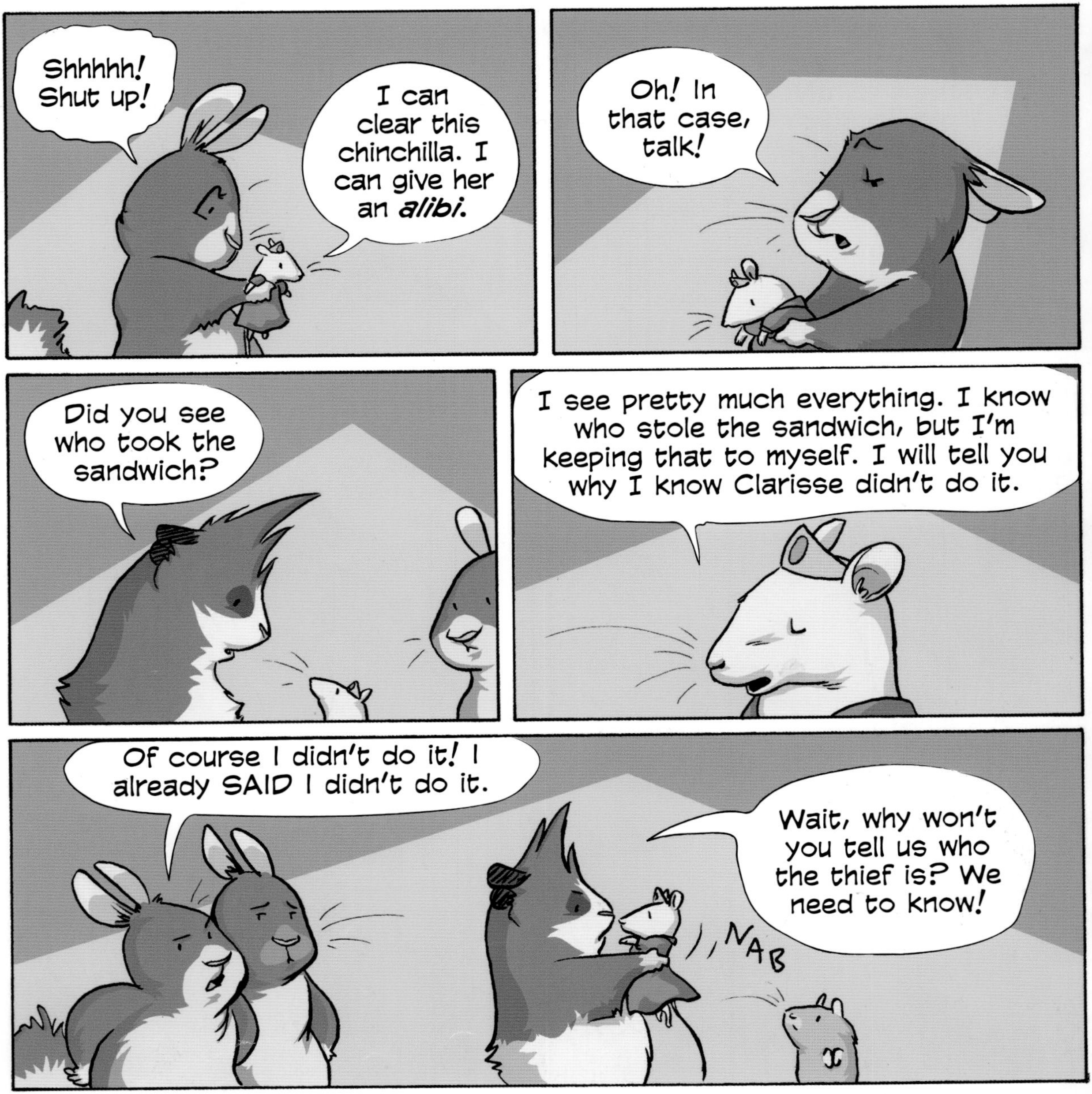
Shhhhh! Shut up!
I can clear this chinchilla. I can give her an *alibi.*
Oh! In that case, talk!
Did you see who took the sandwich?
I see pretty much everything. I know who stole the sandwich, but I'm keeping that to myself. I will tell you why I know Clarisse didn't do it.
Of course I didn't do it! I already SAID I didn't do it.
Wait, why won't you tell us who the thief is? We need to know!
NAB

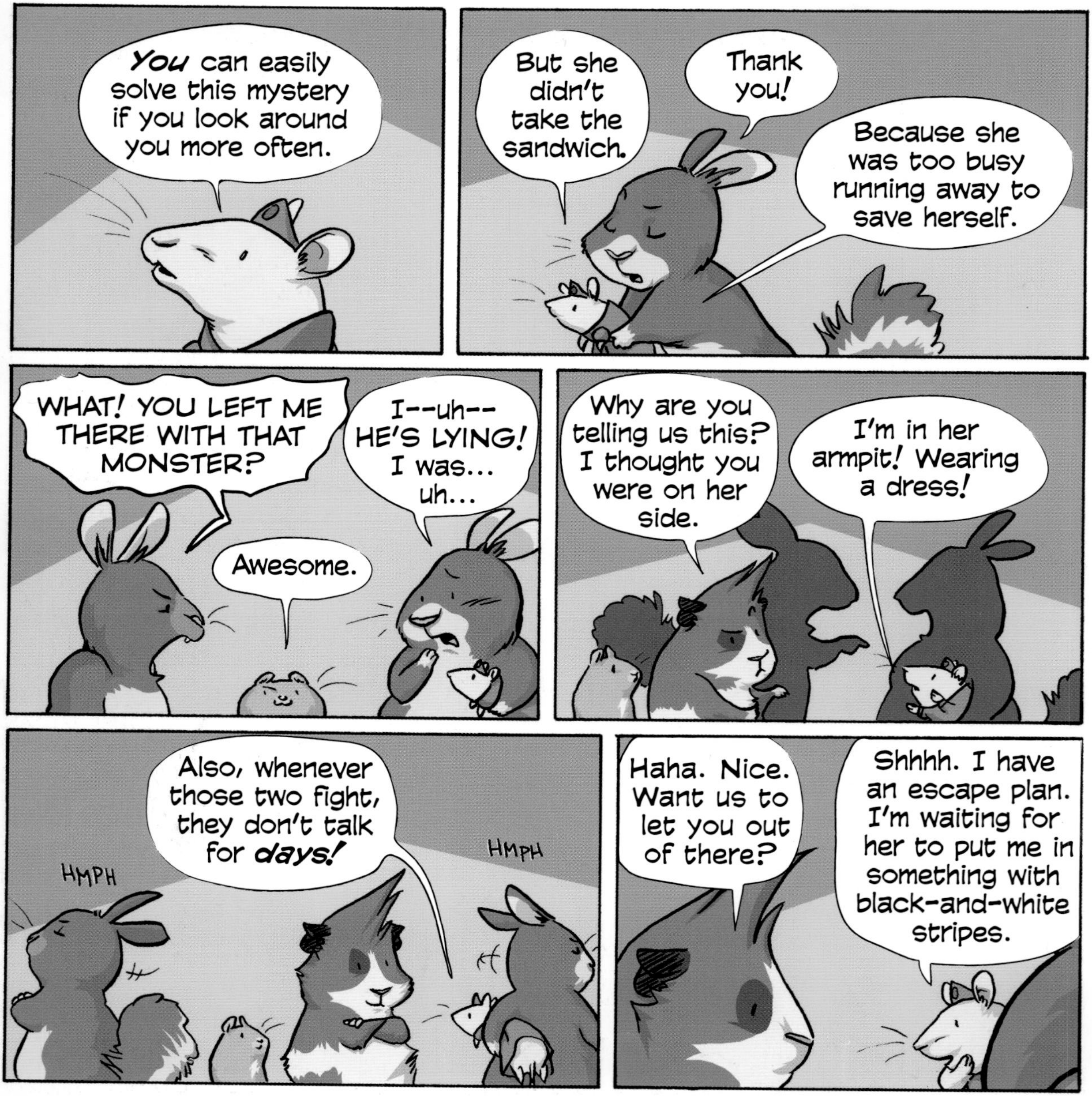

You can easily solve this mystery if you look around you more often.
But she didn't take the sandwich.
Thank you!
Because she was too busy running away to save herself.
WHAT! YOU LEFT ME THERE WITH THAT MONSTER?
Awesome.
I--uh-- HE'S LYING! I was... uh...
Why are you telling us this? I thought you were on her side.
I'm in her armpit! Wearing a dress!
HMPH
Also, whenever those two fight, they don't talk for *days!*
HMPH
Haha. Nice. Want us to let you out of there?
Shhhh. I have an escape plan. I'm waiting for her to put me in something with black-and-white stripes.

We're down to two suspects. Let's go talk to the birds!

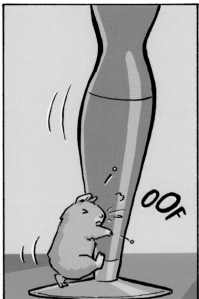

OOF

Hey! I know you!

Well, I'll be.

We've solved it! It must be the birds!

Or maybe *one* bird.

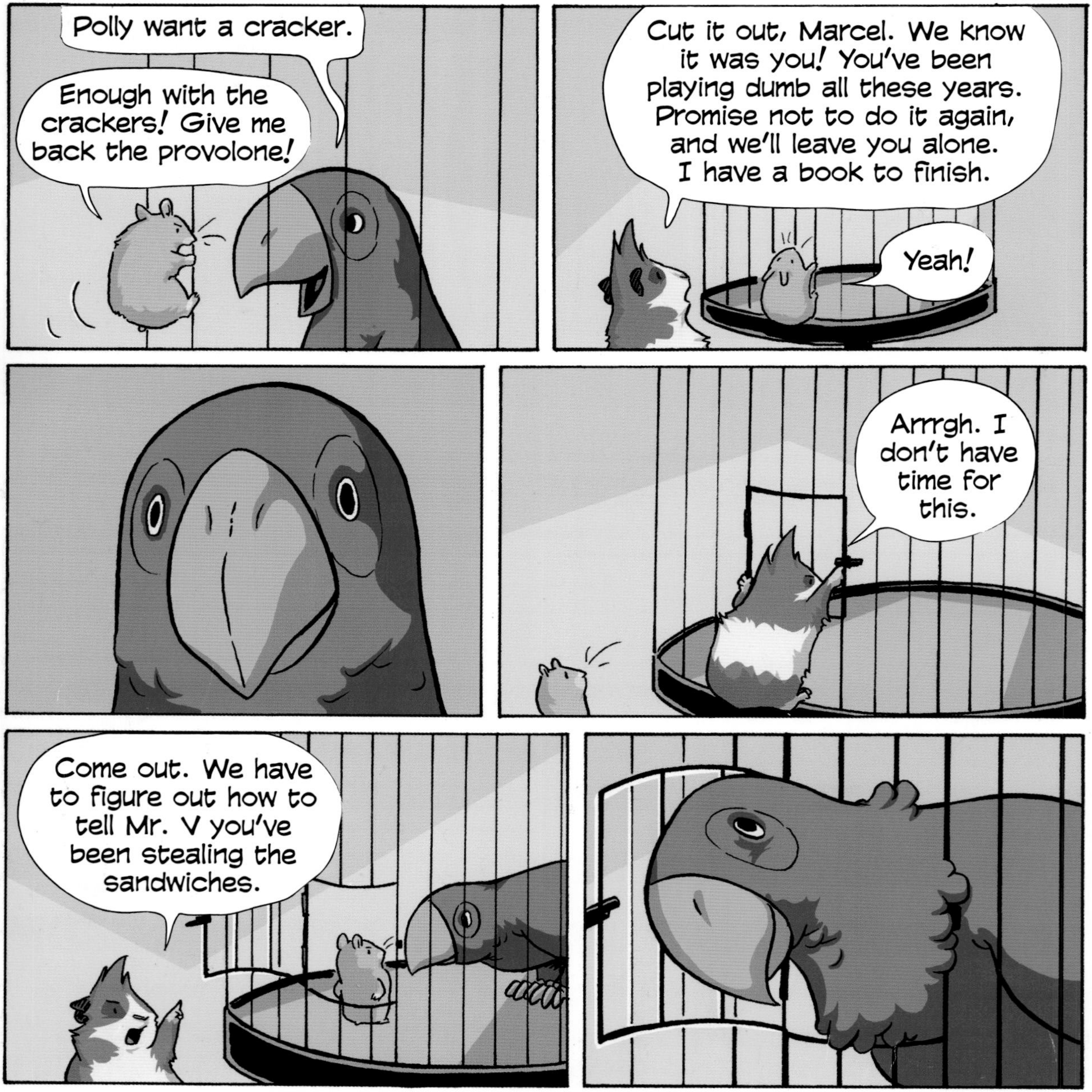
Polly want a cracker.
Enough with the crackers! Give me back the provolone!
Cut it out, Marcel. We know it was you! You've been playing dumb all these years. Promise not to do it again, and we'll leave you alone. I have a book to finish.
Yeah!
Arrrgh. I don't have time for this.
Come out. We have to figure out how to tell Mr. V you've been stealing the sandwiches.

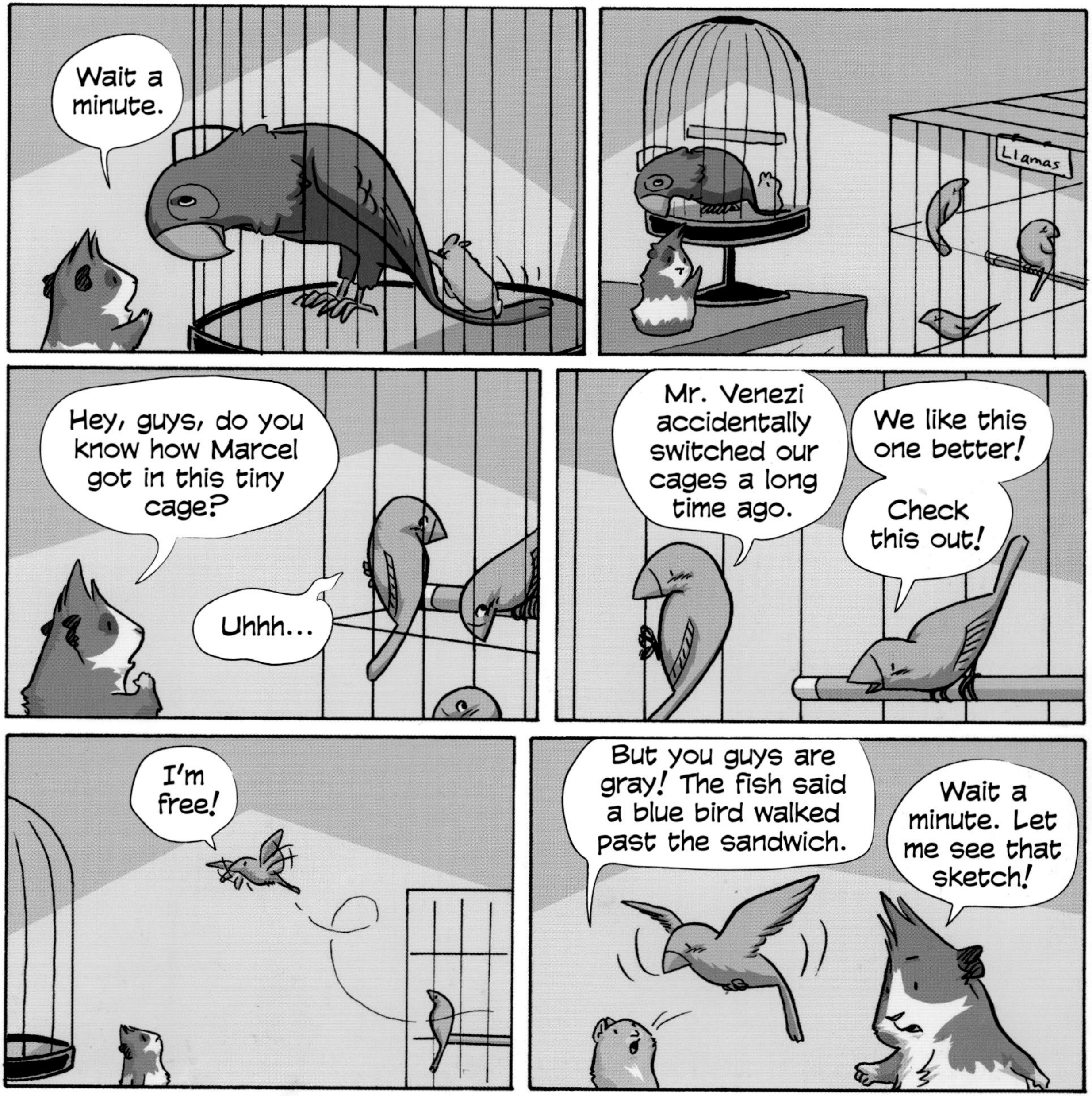
Wait a minute.
Llamas
Hey, guys, do you know how Marcel got in this tiny cage?
Uhhh...
Mr. Venezi accidentally switched our cages a long time ago.
We like this one better!
Check this out!
I'm free!
But you guys are gray! The fish said a blue bird walked past the sandwich.
Wait a minute. Let me see that sketch!

I'VE GOT IT!
I knew I saw that bird before! She comes here every single day, right before lunch! Why didn't I think of this before?!
I SOLVED IT TOO! It was Gerry! Look, the sandwich is in his stomach again. Or is the same sandwich in there? Ew.
That's not a sandwich.
Huh?
Was it worth the taste of that wooden sign to drive me crazy?
GUINEA PI
You'd be surprised how tasty that G was... especially if you imagine it's a hamster on the way down.
Eeeeee.

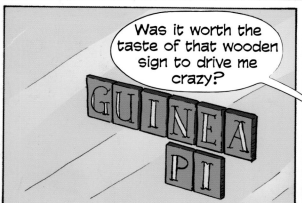

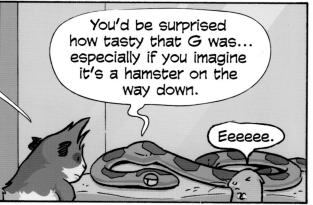

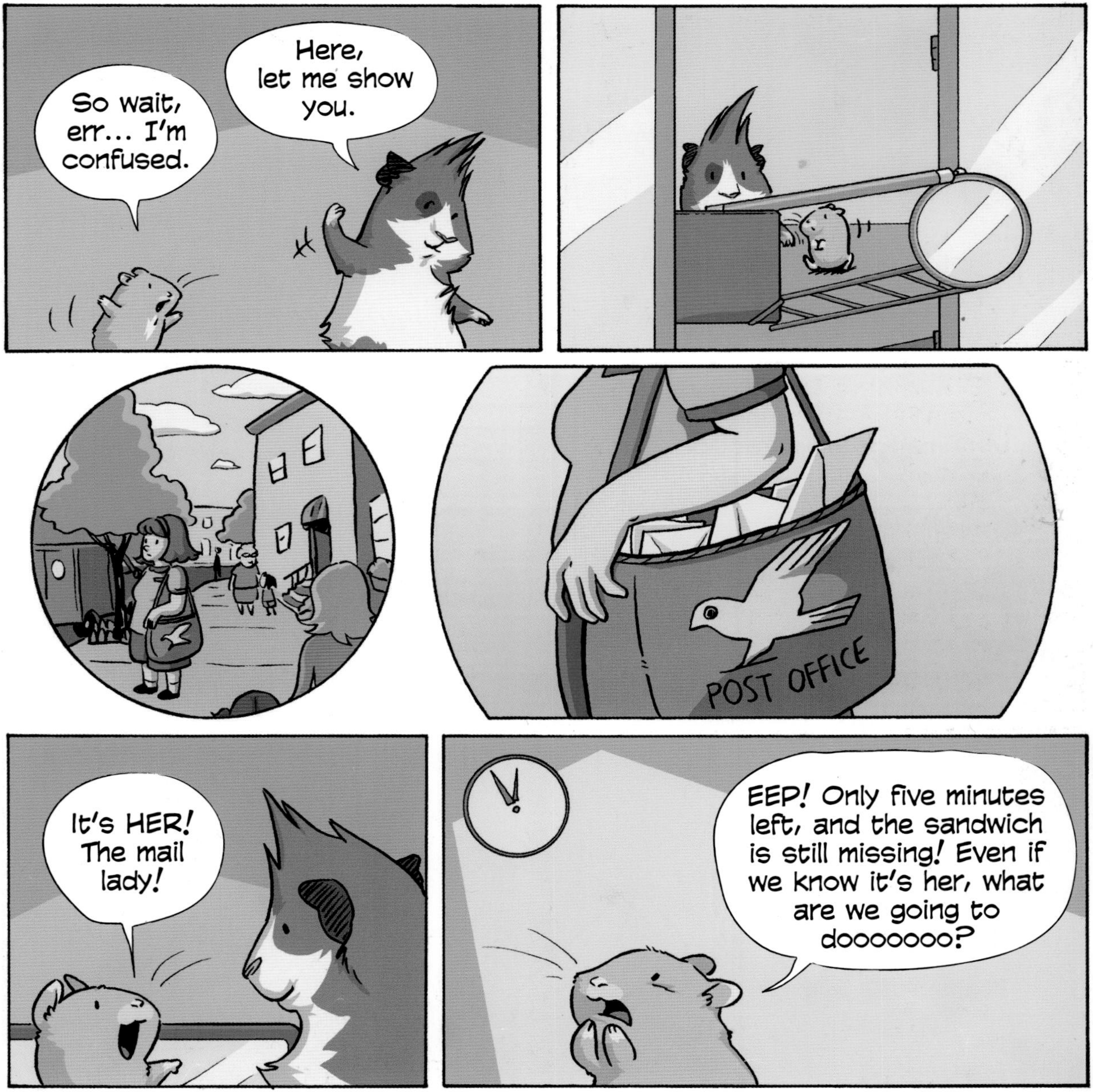
So wait, err... I'm confused.
Here, let me show you.
POST OFFICE
It's HER! The mail lady!
EEP! Only five minutes left, and the sandwich is still missing! Even if we know it's her, what are we going to doooooooo?

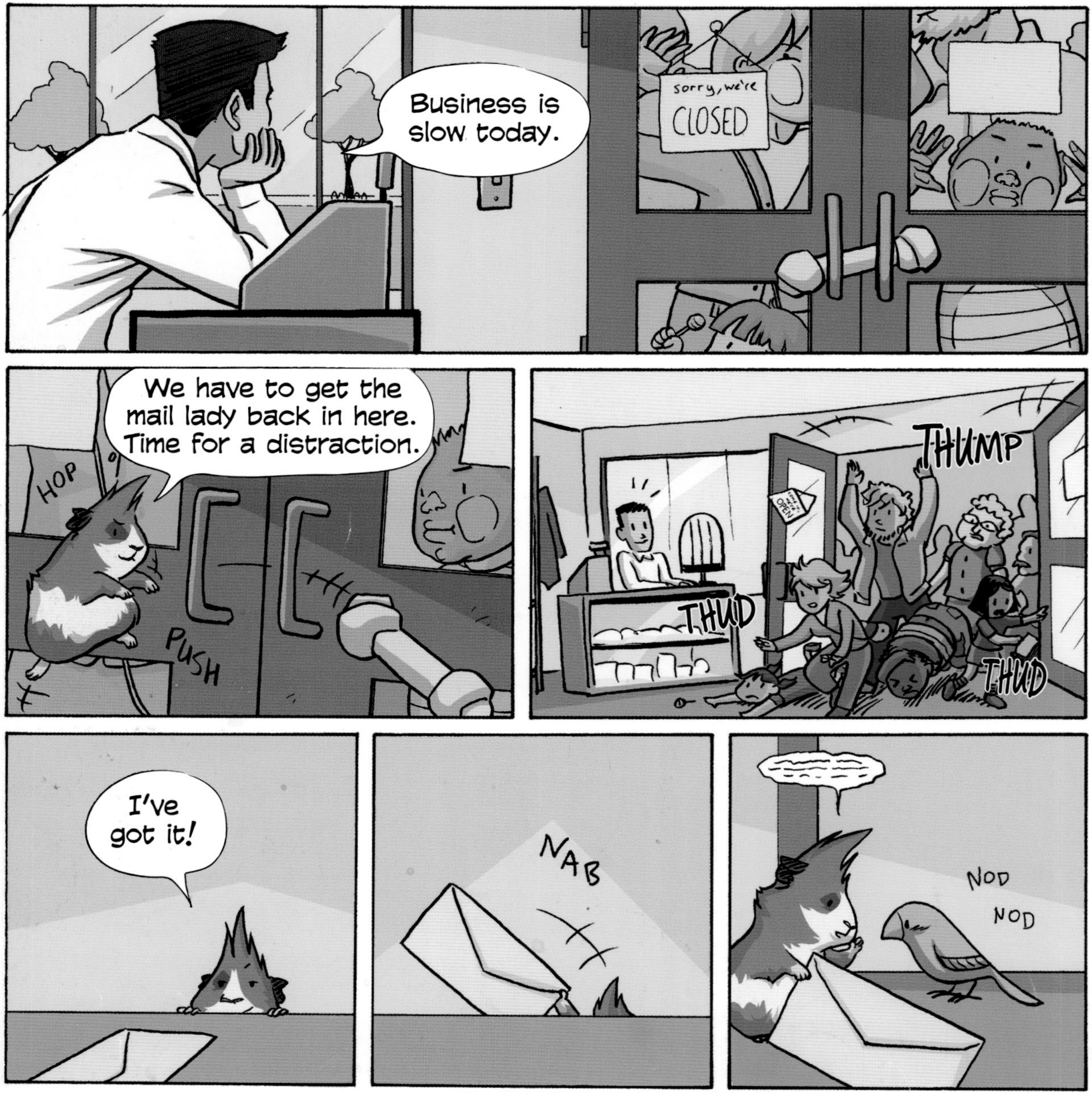
Business is slow today.
Sorry, we're CLOSED
We have to get the mail lady back in here. Time for a distraction.
HOP
PUSH
THUMP
OPEN
THUD
THUD
I've got it!
NAB
NOD
NOD

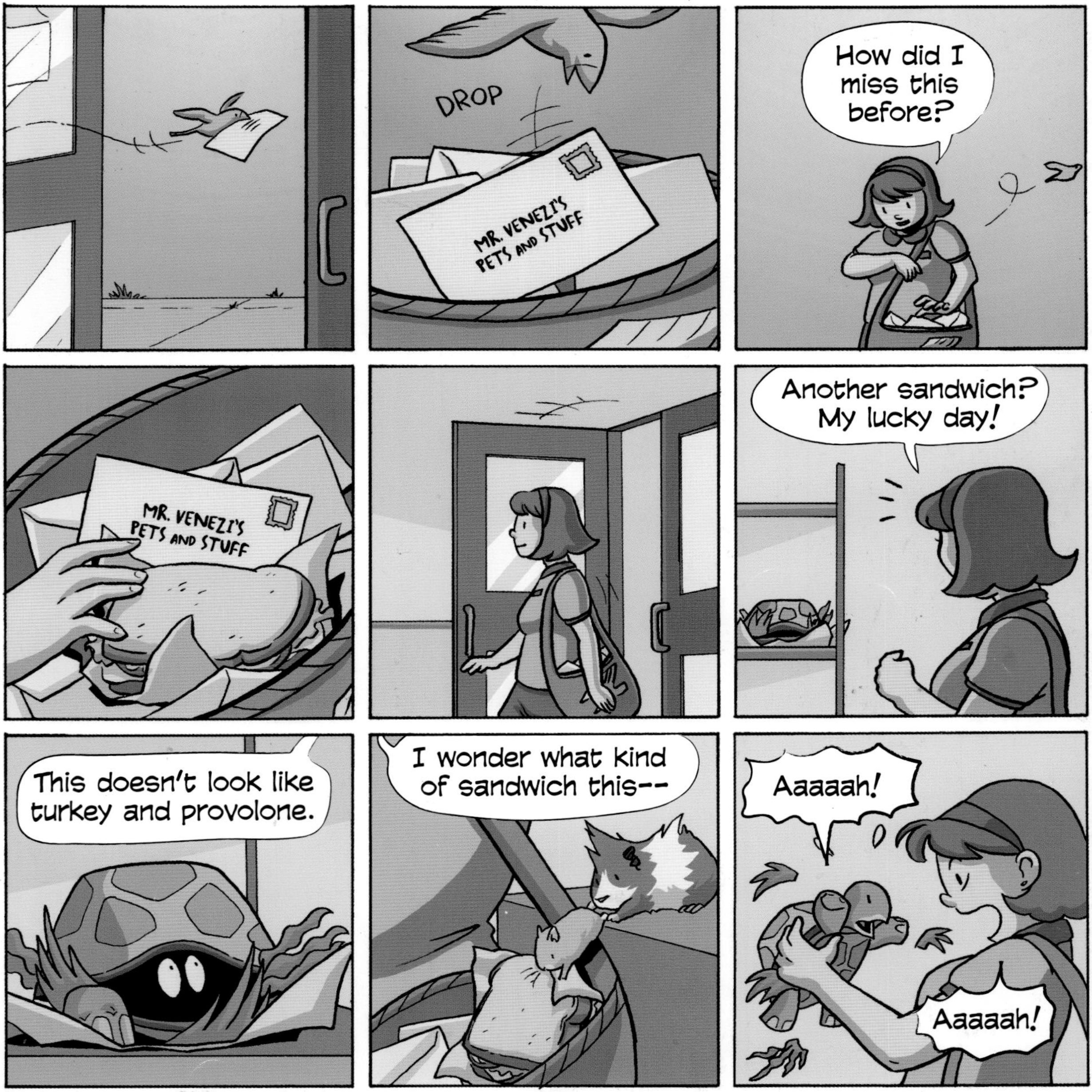
DROP
MR. VENEZI'S PETS AND STUFF
How did I miss this before?
MR. VENEZI'S PETS AND STUFF
Another sandwich? My lucky day!
This doesn't look like turkey and provolone.
I wonder what kind of sandwich this--
Aaaaah!
Aaaaah!

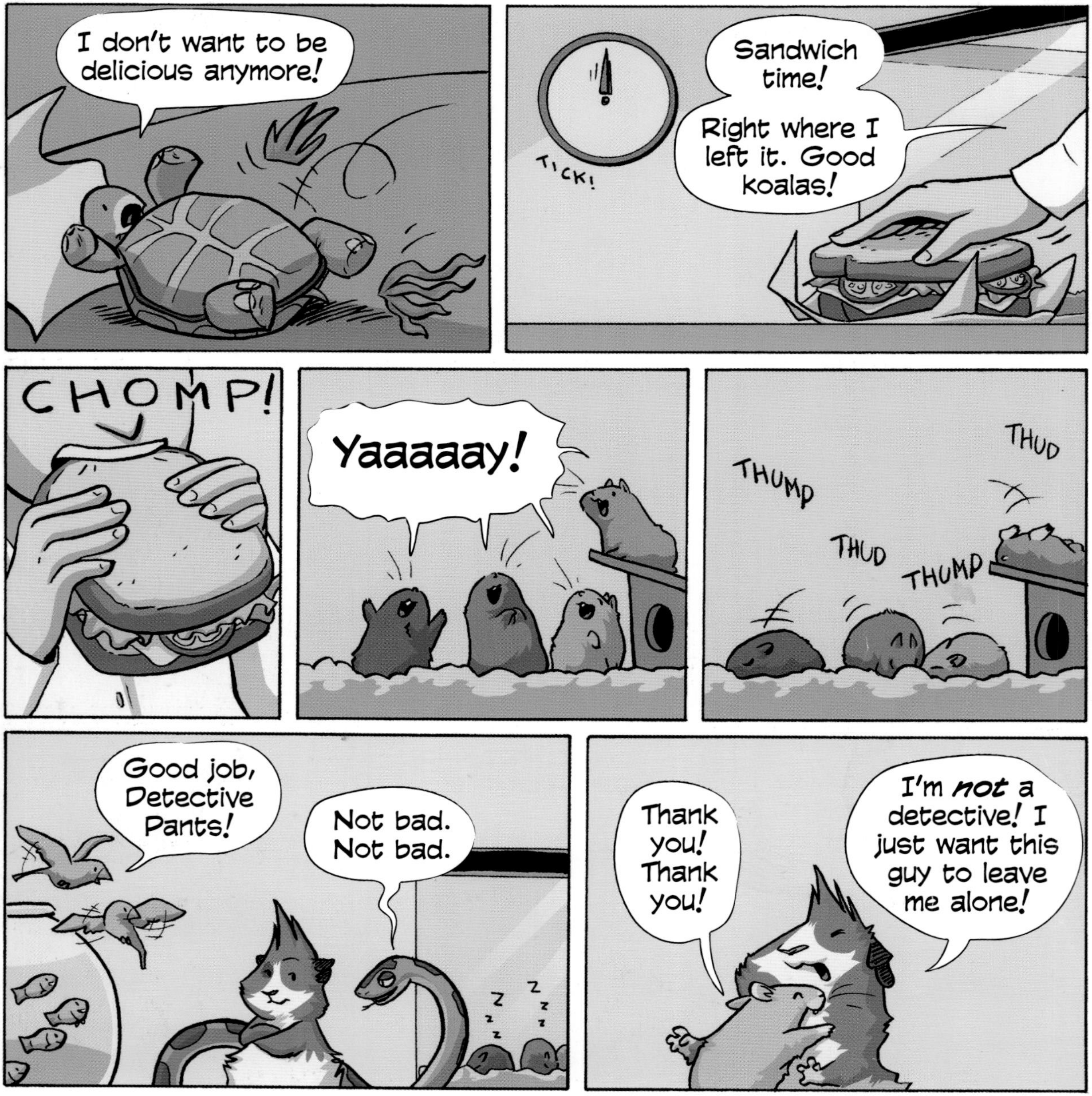
I don't want to be delicious anymore!
Sandwich time!
Right where I left it. Good koalas!
TICK!
CHOMP!
Yaaaaay!
THUMP
THUD
THUD
THUMP
Good job, Detective Pants!
Not bad. Not bad.
Z Z Z Z Z Z
Thank you! Thank you!
I'm ***not*** a detective! I just want this guy to leave me alone!

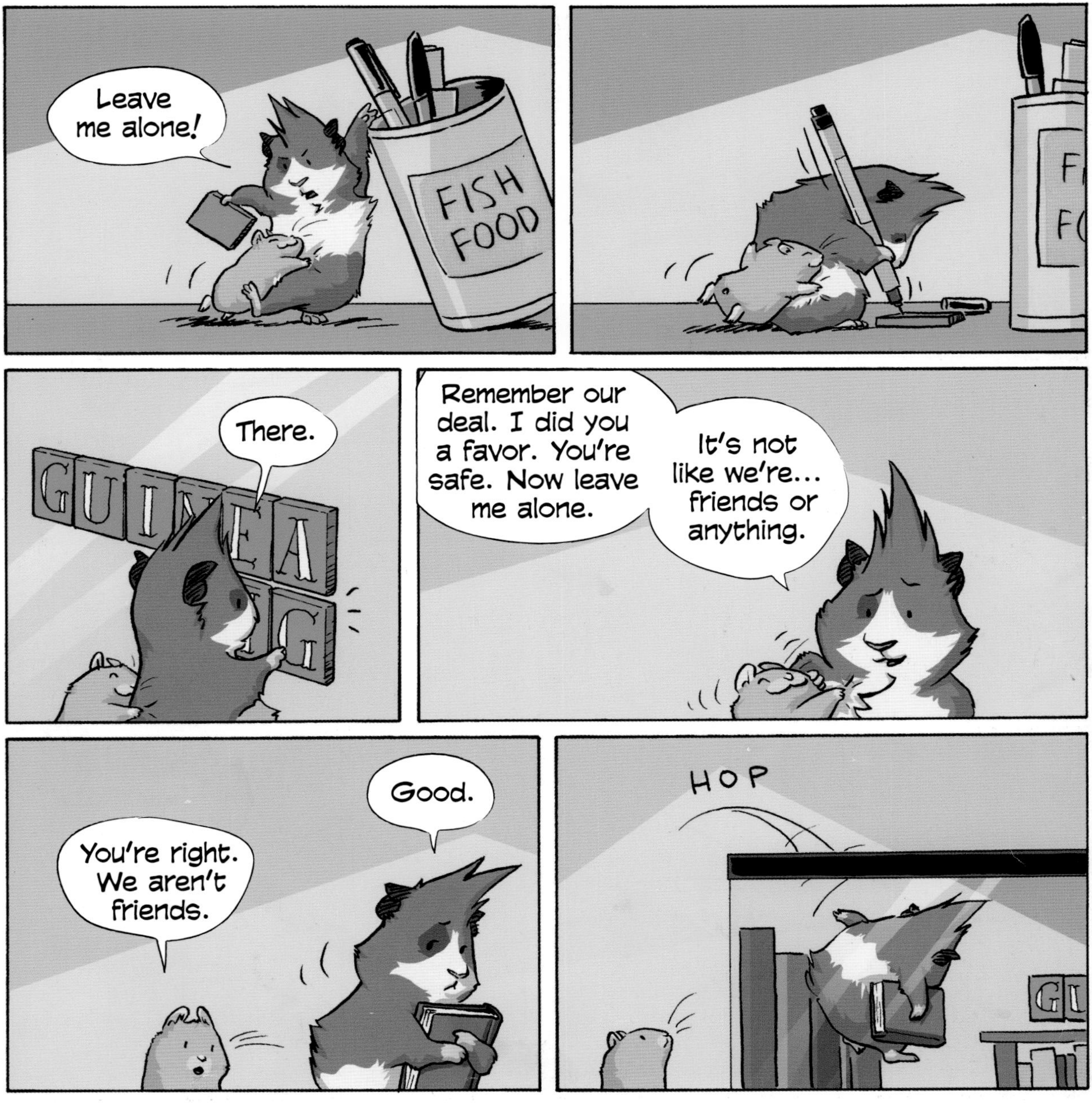
Leave me alone!
FISH FOOD
GUINEA PIG
There.
Remember our deal. I did you a favor. You're safe. Now leave me alone.
It's not like we're... friends or anything.
You're right. We aren't friends.
Good.
HOP

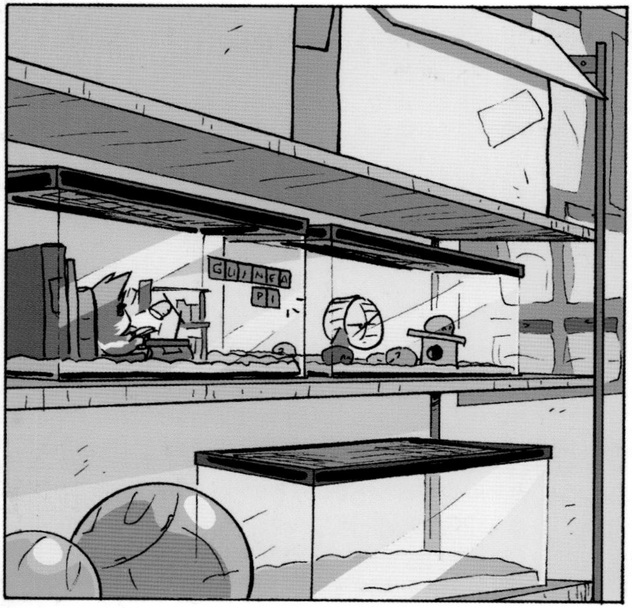
GUINEA
PI

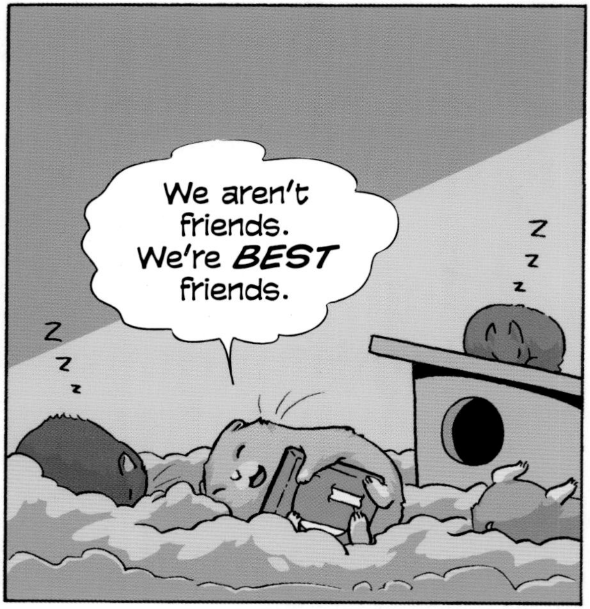
We aren't friends. We're ***BEST*** friends.
Z Z z
Z Z z

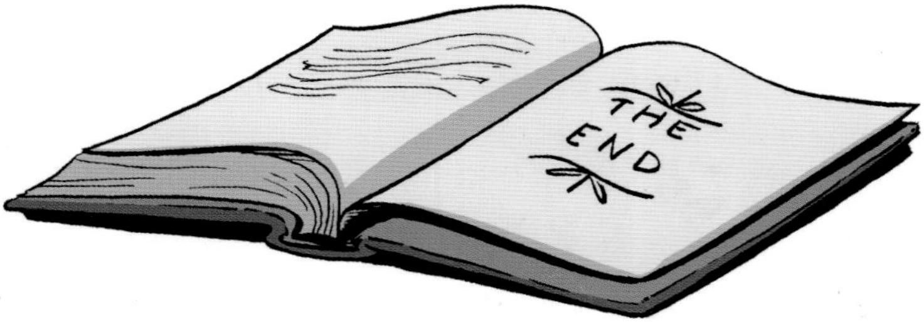
THE END

HAMISHER EXPLAINS...

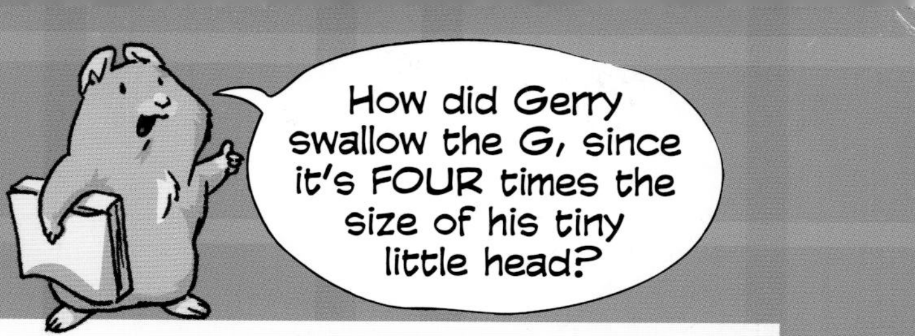
How did Gerry swallow the G, since it's FOUR times the size of his tiny little head?

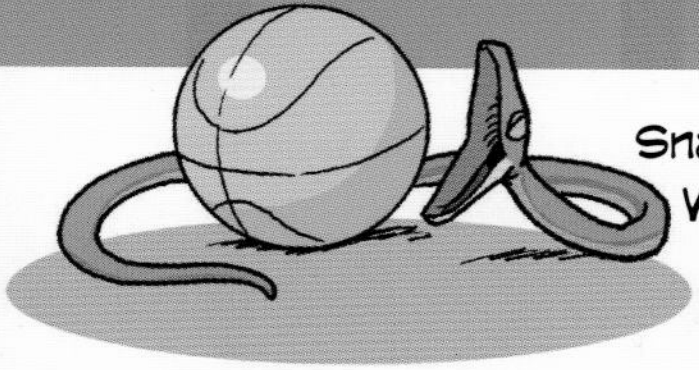

Snakes have jaws that separate. They can open their mouths WIDE to eat HUGE things. It's as if you could open your mouth so wide you could eat a basketball. I'm not sure why you'd want to. Unless it's covered in sunflower seeds. Yum.

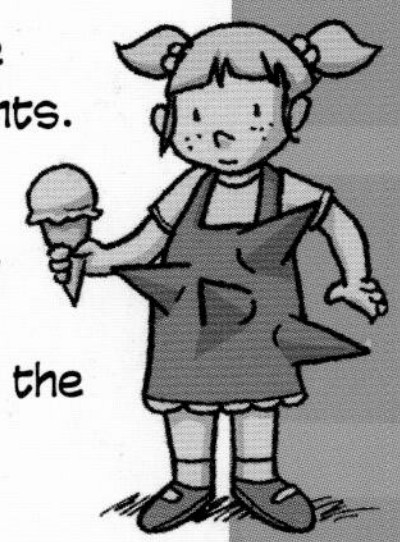

Snakes have HORRIBLE table manners. They never chew their food. It sits inside like a speed bump for three to five days while it slooowly breaks down into nutrients. Imagine if everything you ate showed from the outside!

But all snakes DO have teeth. Poisonous snakes have big Dracula fangs. Normal, boring snakes like Gerry, who is a ***corn snake***, have 200 teeth, all the same size and shape. There are two rows of teeth on the top and one row of teeth on the bottom. He doesn't use them to chew but to make sure food doesn't *escape!*

Snakes are ***carnivores***, which means they ONLY eat meat. ***Omnivores***, such as human beings, eat burgers AND fries. Gerry is called a corn snake because the pattern on his skin looks like corn on the cob. Gerry would never eat corn on the cob.

Snakes are ***dormant*** for a day or two after they eat. *Dormant* means they snooze and relax and don't move at all. Detective Pants and I should have remembered that Gerry can't eat a sandwich every day. Most snakes only eat once a week or so.

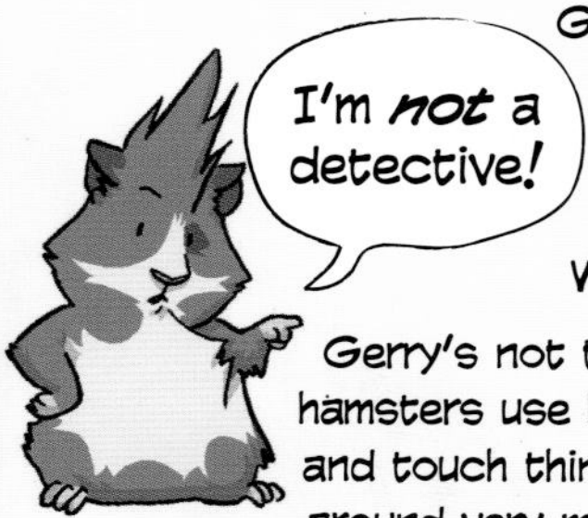
I'm ***not*** a detective!

If snakes slowly dissolve their food, does that mean they don't poop? Nope! ***Snakes poop.*** They don't poop very often. When they do—how can I say this nicely? It's a bit watery.

Gerry's not teasing us when he sticks out his ***tongue***. Humans and hamsters use hearing and sight as our two most busy senses. Snakes smell and touch things. Snakes don't have real ears, and their eyes can't move around very much.

Now, this part is WEIRD! Snakes have noses and nostrils, but they don't use them to smell! They smell with their tongues. Seriously! I mean it! Every time snakes stick out their tongues, they're smelling you. There's a little spot on the roof of a snake's mouth that "smells" stinky things. Gerry is SO not invited to my next birthday party.

Animals **NOT** Appearing in This Book and How to Tell the Difference

RABBITS VS. THREE-TOED SLOTHS

Sloths are found in Central and South America. Sloths only move about one foot every minute. If the old story was called *The Sloth and the Hare* instead of *The Tortoise and the Hare*, the hare would finally win!

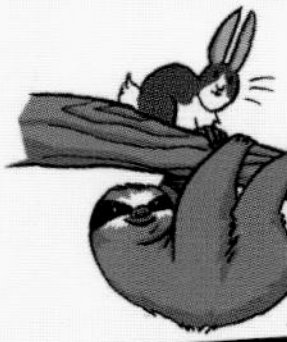

FINCHES VS. LLAMAS

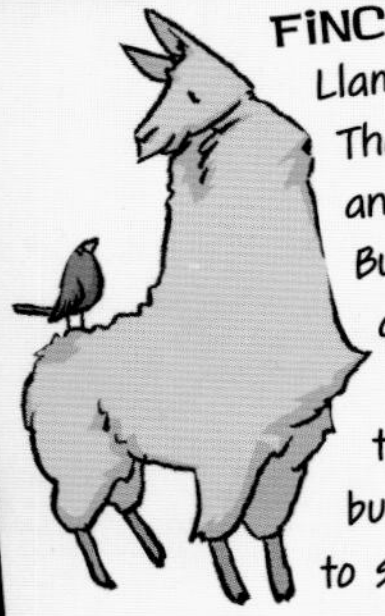

Llamas are furrier than finches. They live in warmer climates, and they aren't good at flying. But finches are a lot louder. Or at least male finches are, since female finches don't sing. No two finches sing the same song, but dads pass similar songs down to sons. The noise llamas make is usually described as "humming." Scientists think it might be because they can't remember the words.

GECKOS VS. MOOSE

Moose is not the plural of *mouse*. They are also not geckos. A moose is not as big as a walrus, but you wouldn't want a 1,600-pound moose in your lap. Luckily, if a moose steps on a gecko's tail, the gecko can "drop" his tail and run away from danger. Then he can regrow the tail later. Pretty handy! (Or tail-y?)

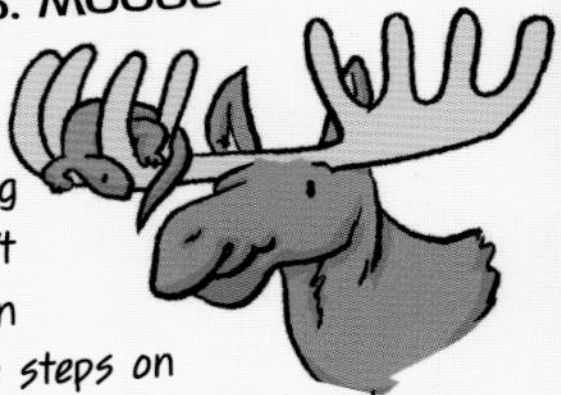

MICE VS. WALRUSES

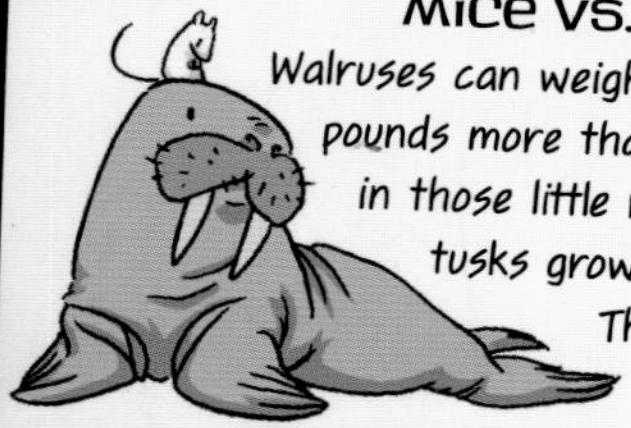

Walruses can weigh up to four thousand pounds more than mice and don't fit in those little running wheels. Walrus tusks grow up to three feet long. The tusks are actually two big teeth.

CHINCHILLAS VS. CAMELS

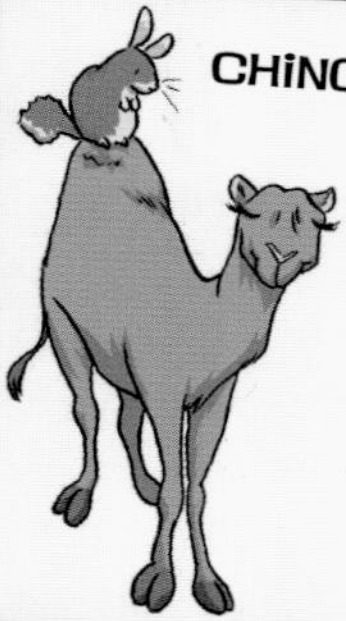

Both chinchillas and camels pee more than twice a year. Mr. Venezi really doesn't know much about pets! Camels are more fun to ride to school.

PARROTS VS. MARMOTS

Marmots are basically large squirrels. They live in chilly places such as the Alps and the Rockies. Parrots like living in warm, tropical places. You'd think marmots would be a lot quieter than parrots, but marmots are known for whistling. Some folks call them whistle pigs.

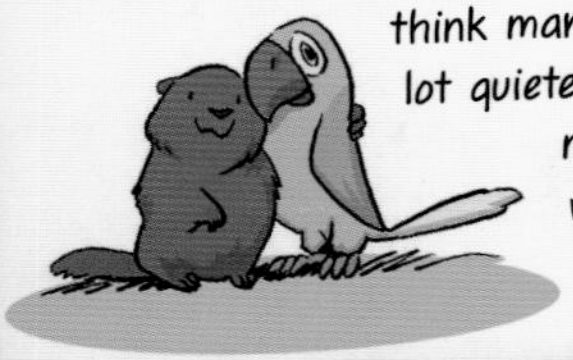

HAMSTERS = KOALAS

Koalas are supercute.
Hamsters are supercute.
There is no difference!

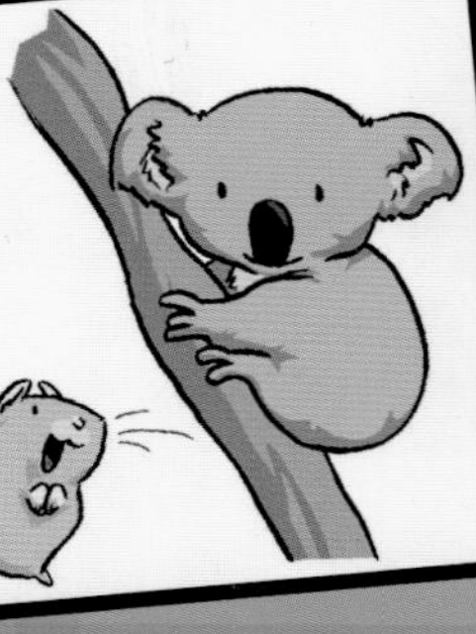

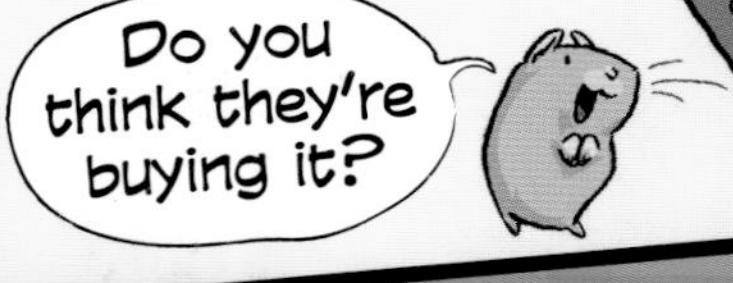
Do you think they're buying it?